THE GHOST OF GRAPE LANE

A DETECTIVE MICHAEL BRADY CRIME THRILLER

MICHAEL BRADY SHORT READS

MARK RICHARDS

AUTHOR'S NOTE

Like all the Michael Brady books, *The Ghost of Grape Lane* is set in and around Whitby, on the North Yorkshire Coast.

As I'm British and the book is set in the UK, I've used British English. The dialogue is realistic for the characters, which means they occasionally swear.

As this is a work of fiction names, characters, organisations, some places, events and incidents are either products of the author's imagination or used fictionally. All the characters in this book are fictitious. Any resemblance to actual persons, living or dead, is purely coincidental.

A note on dates. *The Ghost of Grape Lane* is set in December 2016: as you'll see Brady meets a few old friends, including Ruby. Chronologically it follows *Choke Back the Tears* (set in May 2016) and *The Edge of Truth* (set in September 2016).

I'm still writing *The Edge of Truth*: it will be published in late February 2023.

1

WHITBY: DECEMBER 2016

Michael Brady tapped lightly on his daughter's bedroom door. Waited for the royal summons. "I came to say goodnight, love."

Ash was propped up in bed, reading. "Night, Dad. Are you here in the morning or do I need to fling myself on Fiona's mercy?"

"No, I'm here. I told Frankie I'd be in for ten. I need to do some Christmas shopping. So – "

"You probably haven't heard of it, Dad. There's this thing called Amazon..."

"I'm a traditionalist, Ash. And I'm supporting local shops. So I'll give you a lift to school. Last day of term."

"Not before time. I wish this fog would go. It's been here for weeks. We haven't played hockey since November."

Brady nodded. "You and me both, sweetheart. Frankie and I had fish and chips yesterday. Couldn't even see across the harbour. Anyway, sleep well. Don't read for too long." Brady bent down, kissed her on the forehead. Straightened up again. "Has your Kindle broken?"

"No. Why?"

"That thing... In your hand... It looks suspiciously like a book."

"That's because it *is* a book. *Dracula*."

"You know he landed in Whitby don't you?"

"Thanks, Dad. Good job I've read that chapter."

"Sorry, love. Like I said, don't read too long."

"Dad – "

"What?"

"Jess and I were talking. She said Dracula landed at Tate Hill Pier."

"Did he? I thought it was the East Pier."

"Jess says Tate Hill Pier. That's the one..." Ash gestured at her bedroom window. "...Just down there. So you know what that means, don't you?"

"No. He went up the Hundred and Ninety-Nine Steps didn't he? To St Mary's churchyard?"

"Graveyard, Dad. And that means – if what you say is right: our house was built in eighteen-twenty – Count Dracula went past our front door. Anyway, sleep well, Dad. And if you fall asleep watching football make sure you're holding some garlic."

Brady laughed. Walked over and kissed her again. "You've got too much imagination, Ash. Way too much."

Went downstairs. Found some football on Sky.

Fell asleep 20 minutes later.

2

————

Brady closed the front door behind him. Turned left to walk along Henrietta Street. Said 'good morning' to someone coming out of the kipper smokehouse.

Fortune's Whitby Cured Kippers. Established 1872

Remembered his dad coming home, the kippers wrapped in newspaper. His mother making a face, threatening to put them straight in the bin.

Heard his phone ring.

Glanced down at the display.

Kate.

"You're sure?" she said. "You definitely want to do this? It'd be a lot easier if you all came to me."

Brady laughed. "Good morning, Mike. How are you? That's how sisters start a conversation."

"Sorry, Mike. I'm tense. Christmas. Maddie. Her new boyfriend. I've been awake all night. And now I've added you to my worry list. Tell me I don't need to..."

"You don't. I want to do it. And I've ordered the turkey. The first Christmas in the new house. Besides, I've never cooked Christmas dinner."

"Mike, to the best of my knowledge you've never cooked *anything* except Spag Bol and Chilli."

"A point my daughter has made more than once. So I'm relying on you to give me moral support, Kate."

"Do you want me to come round for an hour? Christmas Eve afternoon? Help you cut crosses in the sprouts? Pour you a gin?"

Brady laughed. "No, I'm good, Kate. Santa's lending me an elf. Siobhan's doing that. Christmas Eve night. Christmas Eve evening if you can say that."

"I thought you said she wasn't staying over?"

"She isn't."

"So she's doing the sprouts, peeling the potatoes and you're sending her home?"

"I'm not *sending* her home, Kate. I've explained. That Christmas morning – the first one in the new house – has to be just me and Ash. And Archie."

"Bloody hell, Mike, you're treading a fine line. Tiptoeing between your daughter and your girlfriend."

"I owe it to Ash."

And Siobhan understands. I think she understands...

"And she's alright with that?"

"She says she is."

"Are you familiar with the word 'keeper,' little brother? Give me six months to lose some more weight before you tie the knot will you?"

"Kate. I'm not... We are not... Just no, Kate."

"Not yet."

"Not – "

"I'm joking, Mike. You're sure you're alright with cooking? You can always do what Dad did. Disappear to the pub and leave it to a woman. Or three women in your case."

"Kate, I have – apparently – a state of the art oven. I've

used it twice. Ash and Siobhan have used it more than I have. This is my moment. *Carpe diem.* Seize the day. Seize the *Christmas* Day. Dinner for six. Ash, Siobhan and me. You, Doug and Lucy. Maddie's still going to her boyfriend's?"

"My little girl, Mike. He's coming here for New Year."

"Are you – "

"Am I going to let them sleep together? What's today? Wednesday. So yes. Tomorrow I'll change my mind. I don't know. I don't want to make the decision."

How many years before I have the same dilemma with Ash?

"You're still going on holiday with Siobhan?"

"Assuming Whitby stays crime free. Four days in Lisbon at the end of February. She says I have to listen to fado. Mournful, sad songs. Never getting what you want. Life grinding you down."

"So songs about police paperwork..."

"Exactly."

3

———

Brady reached the end of Henrietta Street. Passed the Duke of York and The Board. Started walking down Church Street. Stopped, checked they were still in the window. Went into the jet shop.

"Yes, definitely those," he said five minutes later. "Thank you."

The woman behind the counter nodded. "Tear drop. Good choice. Especially if she wears her hair up. Your wife? You want me to gift wrap – "

She hesitated. "Sorry, that was tactless of me."

Brady was used to it now.

Everyone in Whitby knows what happened to Grace...

"Girlfriend then. A new start."

What is it now? Seven months? Girlfriend? I'm too old to have a girlfriend. Partner? No, I'm not ready for that. Not yet...

"Yes, please. I'm hopeless at wrapping. All thumbs."

"You know jet was mourning jewellery don't you? Originally, anyway. Queen Victoria wore it."

Brady nodded. "I do. I was brought up here."

"I know you were. Everyone knows you were. Like I say,

you don't need to introduce yourself. I'm Sadie," she said, holding her hand out. "Boulton in the shop. Turnbull everywhere else."

Long, elegant fingers, dark purple, almost black nail varnish. A rose tattooed on the back of her hand, the leaves reaching up her third and fourth fingers. A stronger grip than Brady had expected.

She bent down, produced some silver wrapping paper from under the counter.

"Saw your picture in the paper the other week, didn't I? That was a bad business. Runswick Bay. Who'd have thought it?" She looked up from the wrapping. "Keeps you in a job though I suppose."

"I suppose so."

But I've had enough. Enough dead bodies for one year...

"Anyway, it's Christmas. Doesn't do to talk about stuff like that."

She handed Brady the small box, wrapped in the silver paper. Smiled at him. "When's her birthday? You know it's unlucky to buy earrings without buying her a necklace?"

Brady laughed. "In the middle of the summer. And I'm taking her on holiday."

"Somewhere hot? Get some sun on your war wound? I read about that n' all." She looked past him and out of the window. "Bloody fog. All my life in Whitby and I've never known a winter like it."

"Tell me about it. My house is at the end of Henrietta Street."

Except she'll know that as well...

"I can't remember the last time I saw the sea. Anyway, thank you. I'll see you in the summer."

Brady gave her his card. Tapped his PIN in. Half-turned to go. Stopped. Had the feeling she wanted to talk.

"Have you always lived in Whitby?" he said.

"Not just Whitby. Spent my whole life here in Church Street haven't I?"

She tilted her head to one side. "Born three doors down the road."

"You must be about my age? Bit unusual to be born at home."

She shook her head. Laughed at him. "I'm nowhere near your age, love. Leapling aren't I? Leap year baby. Only had ten real birthdays in my life. Other years I choose between the twenty-eighth and the first. Depending on which one's a Saturday. So yes, born down the road. Even did my courting in Church Street. Other half lived over there."

She nodded across the road. Brady followed her gaze. "The bookshop?"

"Wasn't a bookshop then. But that's where he grew up. Four of them in one room."

"Four in one room? The place is enormous."

She smiled at him. Brady shivered.

What did Mum used to say? 'Someone's stepped on your grave...'

"Four of them. Two brothers, two sisters. An' you're right. It is a big old place upstairs. Airbnb, they'd have twenty in it. So they all had a room to themselves. Then – " She stopped. "Sorry, I'm keeping you. You must have work to do. Better things to do than listen to my stories."

Brady shook his head. "There's always work to do. Especially paperwork. But no, I'd like to hear it."

Because even though I grew up here I don't know half the stories I should. Because you don't realise they're important until you're older...

Sadie laughed. "You dodging paperwork and me knowing I'll not sell anything in this fog. He lived there with his mam and dad. Brother an' two sisters like I said. Grandad n' all. It's Grandad's money that's paid for it. So one day Grandad takes him an' his brother down to the cellar. Last owner's left a big pile of wood down there. 'Clear it,' Grandad says. 'An' we can put it on the fire for Christmas. Nice n' warm for once.'"

"Must have been dark down there..."

She shrugged. "You tell me. Wouldn't have had electric down there that's for sure. Maybe they had flaming torches. You know, Indiana Jones."

"Raiders of the Lost Firewood? Sorry, it's your story."

"So they start clearing the wood. Carrying it upstairs. Then Davey – he's the younger brother – says, 'what's this?' And there's a well. He nearly goes down it does Davey. An' Grandad finds a pebble and drops it down the well. There's an eternity – other half told me he wished he'd counted the seconds – and then they hear this tiny splash. And then..." She shook her head. "I can still hear him saying it. 'This chill, Sadie. Cold. Coming up out of the well. Cold like you've never felt. Cold to your bones.' So they take the wood upstairs and lock the door. But something's changed. That night Tilly – she's only four, she wasn't down there – she goes into her big sister's bedroom and says, 'Can I sleep with you, Vicky?' And by the end of the week there's four of them – both lads, both lasses – and they're all sleeping in one room. And that's how it stayed."

"Your husband? He thought it had something to do with the well?"

She shook her head. "Didn't think, love, he *knew*. Grandad dies a year to the day after they found it. Couldn't walk across the road fast enough when we got wed and he moved in here."

"So you run the shop together now?"

She shook her head.

"He wasn't cut out for standing behind a counter."

She sighed.

A what-might-have-been expression...

"Then the Barguest Hound came for him."

"The what?"

"The Barguest Hound. Or the Barguest Coach, take your pick."

"I still don't understand."

"He died, love. The story is you can only hear the hound if you're near the end. Or the coach. Pulled by headless horses. The passengers are the skeletons of dead sailors. On their way to pay their respects up at St Mary's. Not sure the poor bugger had time to climb on board, mind. Fell off the pier. Drowned himself."

"I'm sorry."

She nodded. "Me too. Mattie-boy had his faults but he were steady. He used to do the ghost walks in the summer. Easter to Halloween. Always think of him when I walk down Grope Lane."

Brady tried not to laugh. "Grope Lane? You mean Grape Lane?"

"Sheltered life, love? I thought you coppers saw the dark side? Grope Lane they used to call it. No street lights. The ladies of the night with a candle in the window. An' still not a place to visit on a dark night."

"Why not?"

"There's a young girl. Mary Clark, supposedly. She's taking her daddy's dinner to the baker's, her long golden hair flowing behind her. So the baker knows her 'cos she comes every day with her pa's dinner to warm up. He's busy with his bread cakes, so he lets Mary put it in the oven herself – and that's enough.

He hears the most God-awful screams. He turns. Her hair has caught fire. And then the flames are all over. Some say the baker beat the flames out. Some say she ran out into the street screaming, hair still on fire. Either way it's too late. Mary's flesh peels off as she stands there. And if you're in Grape Lane of a night you can still see her. Surrounded by flames, her hair ablaze." She smiled at Brady. Made him shiver a second time. "And they do say you can still smell the burning."

She winked. "He made me do it one time."

"Your husband?"

"Who else? He'd had his hair cut. Made the barber put it in a carrier bag. That night he's doing the ghost walk. I'm hiding down an alley in Grape Lane. Got his hair in a box. When I hear him start telling the story I'm supposed to set light to it. But it's Whitby isn't it? Too bloody windy. The match went out."

She shook her head.

Another what-might-have-been...

"The things we do for love, eh, Michael Brady?"

BRADY WALKED out of the shop. Pulled the collar of his coat up. Watched the fog swirl along Church Street. The damp hanging in the air, the Christmas lights struggling to shine through it.

'Just across the road? The bookshop?'

I should go in. Buy something for Ash. See if I can find her that book by George Clooney's wife. The one she was dropping the world's heaviest hints about.

Brady took a step towards the bookshop.

Stopped. Changed his mind.

Like a shop in Whitby is going to have a book by a human

rights lawyer. Time to do as I'm told. Amazon. If I want it for
Christmas...

Felt someone tap him on the shoulder.

Turned.

"Ruby! What are you doing out in this God-awful
weather?"

"Same as you I should think, Mr Brady. Christmas shopping. Whitby's villains taken a morning off have they?"

"There are no villains, Ruby. Not this week anyway."

She raised her eyebrows. "Or they've made so much
money they're in Spain for the winter. Out of this bloody
fog."

Wrapped up against the cold. Light brown hair still pulled
straight back. A face that once said, 'Life has not been kind to me.'
Now? Not so much...

"You're looking well, Ruby."

"I *am* well. Job's going well. An' I've a new fella n' all.
Well not so much new as second time round. That bloke in
Scarborough. Finally came to his senses. Realised he can't
live without me."

"I'm glad. You look happy. It's working out?"

She shrugged. "Who knows? He's steady enough
though. Must be getting old, Mr Brady. I've had my fill of
mad buggers."

'Steady enough...' Ruby and the woman in the jet shop. I'd
better tell Ash that's what women really want...

"And you're still walking along the cliff to see Alice? Not
in this fog though?"

"Course I am. Why wouldn't I? Specially now there's a
new bairn to tell her about."

"Ross's wife? What did she have?"

"A little girl. Macie. A little stunner. She'd have been
Auntie Alice, Mr Brady..."

He nodded. "She would, Ruby. You just take care when you're going to see her. We've had one body at the bottom of the cliffs. We can do without another."

Ruby laughed. "I'll take my chances with the cliffs. It's Constance that terrifies me."

"Constance? Who's Constance?"

Ruby shook her head. "Fog like this? You need to read up on your ghosts, Mr Brady. Constance de Beverley."

"Not you as well, Ruby. I've had Ash frightening me with Dracula. The lady who owns the jet shop – "

"Sadie? Tell you about the book shop did she? Her other half? Good job I stopped you going in."

"She did. And Grape Lane. So you may as well complete the set. Who's Constance de Beverley?"

"Who *was,* you mean. She was a nun. A young nun. And she fell in love with a handsome knight. And did what we all do after a few rum n' blacks. Broke her vows of chastity."

"When's this?"

"I don't know, do I? When it was being built I suppose. 'Cos they bricked the poor lass up in the walls of Whitby Abbey."

"That's a bit drastic."

"Always the bloody same isn't it? The woman that pays. So they do say that on a still, dark night you can hear poor Constance pleading for mercy. *And* early morning in this fog..."

"You've heard her?"

Ruby nodded. Drew a cross over her heart. "Clear as a bell. Swear to God."

Brady shook his head. "You're worse than my daughter, Ruby. Like I say, you just take care on that cliff top. And have a lovely Christmas with Macie."

"I will, don't you worry. An' I know you're too shy to ask,

Mr Brady. So yes, you *can* give me a Christmas kiss. Right in the middle of Church Street n' all. Should set some tongues wagging."

Brady laughed. Leant forward. Kissed her on the cheek. "Happy Christmas, Ruby."

"Mind, Mr Brady, I heard you were getting married again."

Brady shook his head. "Whitby gossip, Ruby. Put two and two together and make six hundred."

"But we're standing across from the jewellers. An' you've got a bag in your hand..."

"We are, Ruby. And I have. But it's jet, not diamonds. And I'd have to ask my daughter's permission..."

Ruby winked at him. "Tricky things, teenage daughters. You have a lovely Christmas, Mr Brady."

"I will, Ruby, I will."

Brady watched her walk down Church Street. Half a dozen steps and she was swallowed by the fog.

4

"Christmas shopping all done, boss?"

"If you want the truth, Frankie, the answer's no. I was going to get it done yesterday. I'll have to wave the white flag and surrender to Amazon – "

"Or leave early. Those Sunday mornings clearing up the mess at Runswick must be worth some time off."

"Too late, Frankie. I should have taken your advice. Stayed a sergeant and collected the overtime. I'd be having Christmas in Barbados."

"Except you've got the new house. You're definitely cooking Christmas dinner?"

"Don't you start, Frankie. I was barely out of the house yesterday before Kate phoned me. Ash has put 'indigestion tablets' on her Christmas list. Twice. Anyway, I'm organised. Or I would be organised if I hadn't spent the morning listening to ghost stories. I bumped into Ruby. She was telling me about a nun bricked up in the walls of the Abbey."

"Did she tell you about the lighthouse keeper?"

"Bloody hell, Frankie, not you as well. All I need is Dave

telling me the harbour's haunted by some poor bastard who choked to death on a bacon sandwich and I've got a full house. Except the lighthouse keeper, obviously. But I assume – seeing as Whitby's a crime-free zone and all our paperwork is filed under 'fuck it, do it in the New Year' – that you're going to tell me. Let me get a coffee."

"THE WEST PIER," Frankie said five minutes later.

"*My* West Pier? The one I can see from the house?"

"The very same. It's blowing a hoolie. Waves coming over the pier. Rain's vertical off the sea."

The West Pier where Jimmy Gorse tried to kill me...

" – And the lighthouse keeper's in town. Buying his Christmas presents maybe... Looks at the pier. Sees the lighthouse isn't lit. So he gets his lamp. Battles his way along the pier. By the time he reaches the lighthouse he's soaked to the skin. Water pouring off him. But he makes his way up the stairs. Lights the lamp. Saves the ships. Then he's coming back down the steps."

"What happened?"

"He slipped. Stone steps. They're wet. All the water that's dripped off him on the way up. So he slips on the top step. Hits his head on every single one on the way down."

"And you're going to tell me his ghost haunts the lighthouse?"

She shook her head. "The pier. Straight across from your house. And on a dark night – especially when the sea's coming over – you can still see his lamp. As he makes his way along the pier."

"How come you know so much?"

Frankie laughed. "Everyone in Whitby knows the stories. Like Shakespeare said, there are more things in

Heaven and Earth than are dreamt of in your philosophy, Inspector Brady."

Brady shook his head. "No there aren't, Frankie. There's *evidence* in my philosophy. No vampires, no werewolves, no ghouls, no ghosts. Just cold, hard evidence. Especially ten days before Christmas. And I'm having some time off. Christmas dinner. A solitary drunk on Boxing Day. That'll do for crime. And with that I'm off to the butcher's. Bacon, pigs-in-blankets and ten minutes idle gossip about football."

"If you can find the butcher's in the fog."

"Right." Brady shook his head. "I could barely find Church Street this morning. Or my car. Let's hope no-one trips over a body up on the Moors. It'll be a bloody long walk."

The phone rang on Brady's desk. "Kershaw, I expect. Telling us we've all been given a Christmas bonus."

Detective Sergeant Frankie Thomson snorted. Made a gesture. Only used one finger.

"Boss?"

A single word.

That was all it took.

Brady knew instantly.

Her tone of voice.

Felt the familiar sensation in his stomach.

Billy and Sandra all over again.

'We've had a call. Out at Horkome. The caller says he took a parcel round to his next door neighbours. Husband and wife. They're both dead. Or he says they're dead.'

'How's he know they're dead?'

'They're tied to the fireplace.'

"What is it, Sue?"

"Bagdale Hall, boss. They've found a body. They say it's murder."

I daren't ask. Here goes Christmas...

"How do they know it's murder?"

"Because the bedroom's decorated with blood. And the back of his head is missing..."

5

"I'll get the car," Frankie said.

"No. Leave it. Fog like this? We'll walk. It can't be more than five minutes."

"Not exactly *The Sweeney*, boss. John Thaw and Dennis Waterman doing a high-speed chase through London. Michael Brady and Frankie Thomson walking..."

"It's Whitby, Frankie. And the fog's getting thicker. You'll need your big coat..."

BAGDALE HALL LOOMED up out of the murk. Brady just made out Anya's scene of crime van in the car park.

"Sixteenth century," Frankie said. "Built for Henry VIII's Serjeant-at-Arms."

Brady forced a smile. "Probably what we need. Someone to keep order. I don't want this turning into a circus."

He pushed the heavy wooden door open. Shook hands with the manager. Balding, overweight, visibly nervous.

Made the introductions.

"One of your chambermaids found him?"

"Yes. Rachel. Mr Hodge always comes down for breakfast. *Came* down for breakfast. I'm sorry."

"He'd stayed here before?"

"Every time he was in Whitby. Some sort of engineer. Checking the harbour wall. Twice a year usually."

"So your staff knew him? What was his first name?"

"Joseph. Joe, people called him. And we like to think we know *all* our regular visitors, Mr Brady. He'd told us he had a meeting at nine."

"At the harbour?"

A nervous nod. "So he wanted breakfast for seven-thirty. When he hadn't appeared by eight – and he didn't answer his phone. I asked Rachel..."

"Where is she now?"

"She's in one of the meeting rooms. Someone's with her. We've given her a brandy."

Brady smiled. "You've done the right thing. Could you take Detective Sergeant Thomson to her? I'll find my way upstairs. What room is it?"

Not that I won't be able to find it...

"Twenty-six?"

Two thirteens...

"Along the corridor. Right at the end. On your left."

Brady nodded. "Thank you. And when I come down Sergeant Thomson and I will check the CCTV. The car park and the entrance should do it."

The manager shook his head. Looked down at the carpet. "I'm sorry. It's not been working properly. The fog. The damp..."

"So there's no CCTV for yesterday?"

"No. Not for a few days. The engineer was coming. It's a company in Middlesbrough. He had to turn round."

Don't tell me. The fog was too thick.

One-nil to the murderer...

BRADY PULLED the pale blue hood of the crime scene suit over his head. Stepped carefully into room 26.

Maroon patterned carpet. White walls. TV mounted on the wall. Big double bed. White quilt, white sheets. Ornate bedposts. Old fashioned wardrobe. Bedside table. Bedside light still on...

"How are you doing, Anya? And how did you get here so quickly?"

The Scene of Crime Officer was kneeling over the body. She turned, looked up. Dark brown eyes, a wisp of hair so black it was almost dark blue escaping from her hood.

"I was driving past, boss. Coming back from another job. Quarter of a mile away when I got the call."

"You got enough of everything? Evidence markers and all that?"

"I'm good. The other job wasn't much more than finger-prints. Out at Lealholm. Over the Moors. That's a drive you don't want to do in the fog."

Brady heard a noise. Turned. Saw the police photographer, camera already in his hand. "Paul. Morning. Give me a minute will you? Then I'll leave you and Anya to it. There's not a lot of room in here. Especially..."

Brady looked down at Joe Hodge's body. Dark hair. Naked from the waist up. Tracksuit bottoms, bare feet. Right arm up. Right leg slightly bent.

And like Sue said, the back of his head missing.

Technically, not missing.

Spread evenly around the room...

The blood soaking into the carpet. A thick carpet. It'll need replacing...

Smelled the familiar metallic, rusted-iron smell of the blood. Looked around the room.

Walls, sheets, lampshade.

'Decorated' is right. Or that painter. Jackson Pollock?

The walls as his canvas. Painted with Joe Hodge's blood.

Even the TV...

Forced himself to look back at the body.

About my age. The same height as me? Hard to tell. Looks in good shape...

Brady shook his head. "Twenty years of dead bodies," he said out loud. "This one's spectacular. What is it, Anya? Ten pints? Half his blood must be on the walls – "

"And the rest soaking into the carpet? A little blood goes a long way, boss."

"It's still a mess. Poor bugger. Any immediate thoughts?"

"Apart from the fact that someone hit him very, very hard?" She shook her head. "Two, maybe three blows. My guess is the first one wasn't fatal. But I'm guessing."

"You want to guess at time of death?"

"Definitely not. I'll wait for the expert. Geoff must be on his way."

"OK, I'll leave you and Paul in peace."

Brady walked out of the room. Stripped off his crime scene suit. Paused. Looked back at the room door. Heard Paul's camera clicking. A muted comment from Anya he didn't catch.

'Someone hit him very, very hard...'

Saw the blood spattered across the TV. Had an image of wiping blood off the screen before he watched football. Felt ashamed of himself.

And knew he'd missed something.

Couldn't think what.

Shook his head in frustration and went to find Frankie.

Let's see what Rachel has to say. Not much I expect...

'*She's in one of the meeting rooms.*'

Brady walked down the corridor. Saw a door open. Frankie come out. Hold her hand up.

"Someone's with her. Poor kid, she's only nineteen. Still lives with her mum. She's not in a good way."

"What did she say?"

Frankie shook her head. "What we expected her to say. The manager asked her to go up. Knock on the door, take Hodge some coffee. She knocks, no answer. Goes back and tells the manager. He says, 'knock again. He's got a meeting.' Still no answer. She daren't go back and ask the manager again. So she uses her key – "

"The door's locked?"

Frankie nodded. "Locked. Nothing unusual. She said she didn't scream. Said she'd seen films where chambermaids find bodies. 'They always scream,' she said. She didn't scream, didn't drop the coffee."

Brady nodded. "Something for her to hang on to. You're letting her go home? I'll send someone to take a statement."

"I'll do it," Frankie said. "She's a good kid. Better me than Jake or Dan. How was it upstairs? You need me to go and look?"

Brady shook his head. "Geoff's just gone up. I passed him on the stairs. Joe Hodge is dead. Blood all over the room. Soaking into the carpet. According to Anya, 'someone hit him very, very hard.'"

"Time of death?"

"I'll leave that to Geoff. I'll talk to him and Anya when they're finished. Let's get back. Find out everything there is to find out about the unfortunate Mr Hodge."

Frankie hesitated. "You mind if I go up there, boss?"

"It's not pretty."

"Like I said that time at Horkome, I didn't sign up for 'pretty.' And I know Paul's a bloody good photographer. But I'd rather see it with my own eyes."

The difference between watching it live and seeing it on TV...

"No problem. I'll have another word with our very-nervous manager. Find out why he let Rachel open the door instead of doing it himself. One other thing, Frankie. There was no CCTV. The fog, according to the manager."

Frankie raised her eyebrows. "You think the killer knew?"

Brady shook his head. "I'd like to think so. Because it's a remarkably small pond to fish in. The manager. Maybe two or three other people in the hotel. The engineer who turned back, the – "

"The engineer who *says* he turned back."

Brady nodded. "Fair point. But easy enough to check. He'll have a time sheet. The van might have some sort of tracking device. Get Dan Keillor onto it. The engineer, his boss, the person who took the call in Middlesbrough. That's probably it. Ten minutes and they're ruled out. No, I don't think the killer knew. I think he got lucky."

6

'*I was busy, Mr Brady. Christmas bookings. Only me and Mrs Firth in the office. How was I to know he'd been murdered?*'

Brady shook his head.

Suppose Ash had a holiday job? Suppose that happened to her?

Looked up as Anya knocked on his door. Gestured for her to sit down.

"What've you got for me, Anya?"

She reached into her handbag, found her trademark yellow pencil. Wound her hair round it. Flipped the pencil over, used it to secure her hair.

Is that in a woman's genes? Ash can do it. Siobhan. Frankie. I could grow my hair, live to a hundred and all I'd do is spend sixty years dropping pencils on the floor...

"I've got... Honestly, boss? I've almost got *too* much. You saw the crime scene. The bedroom's like a text-book. Like it's been laid out for an exam. Where you come out of the exam room, go to the pub and say, 'Right, like we're ever going to see one as helpful as that in real life...'"

She shook her head. "But we did. Where do you want me to start?"

"Wherever you like. Wherever makes most sense. You want coffee or anything? This sounds like a long conversation."

Anya shook her head. "I'm good, thanks. I've decided to live a long and healthy life. Our coffee machine plays no part in that."

Brady laughed. Reached for his cup. "Too late for some of us. Fire away."

"First things first. The murderer came in through the door."

"Definitely not the window?"

"Not unless he was Count Dracula. No sign of the window being opened. No tell-tale footprints in the flowerbed – "

"Agatha Christie would be disappointed."

"She wound up in Harrogate, boss, not Whitby. But you're right. I asked Jake to check when he came. No marks of a ladder. Nothing."

"No connecting doors with the next bedroom?"

"This is Bagdale Hall, boss. Not the Premier Inn."

"So the killer knocked on the door and Joe Hodge climbed out of bed and opened it?"

Anya nodded. "I think so. I know so. Or I'm ninety-nine per cent certain. And so is Geoff."

"Then what?"

"Alright, I'm moving more into the realm of speculation here. But I'm still right."

Brady looked at her.

Black jeans, a black leather jacket she could have borrowed off Frankie. Completely focused...

Wondered how long someone so bright would stay in

Whitby. Wondered for the hundredth time what had brought her to the town in the first place.

"Go on..."

"Hodge opens the door. Turns his back on the killer."

"You're sure?"

She nodded. "The position of the blows. I've discussed it with Geoff. The first one is on the side of his head. We think Hodge opens the door. Walks back into the room. Then he turns. Maybe the killer said something. That's when he hit him."

Jimmy Gorse knocking on Carl's door. Exactly the same. The first blow knocks him down. Then Gorse goes to work...

"So he's down on the floor?"

"He is. Probably still conscious, but dazed. Definitely can't defend himself. We think two more blows to the back of his head. Impossible to say which one was fatal."

Brady briefly closed his eyes. Saw Joe Hodge lying on the bedroom floor. Track suit bottoms. No top. Bare feet. "What about the murder weapon? What's he hit him with?"

Anya nodded. Smiled to herself. "And this is where it gets interesting. Geoff will confirm all this for you. But I'd say that Mr Hodge was hit with a medieval cudgel."

Brady stopped making notes. Stared at her. "Say that again."

"I'd say he was hit with a medieval cudgel. Or something very similar."

"You're talking of one of those weapons knights used? A joust on *Game of Thrones*? They haven't settled it on horseback so now they're on foot?"

"You're thinking of a mace, boss. I'm talking something his squire might have carried. Wooden. Maybe fourteen or sixteen inches long. Reassuringly heavy. An iron band at the end. Spikes sticking out. The sort of thing you'd use in hand-to-hand combat. That would end a tavern brawl with one blow."

Brady shook his head. Looked out of the window. Saw nothing but the fog.

"So Joe Hodge is hit at least twice – probably three times – with what you're calling a medieval cudgel. You and Geoff are sure about that?"

Anya nodded. "As sure as we can be. Geoff's doing the post-mortem now."

"So why are you convinced the murder weapon's been borrowed from Jaime Lannister's squire?"

"Because there's damage from a blunt object. But fragments of his skull have got puncture wounds as well. I went to a lecture at the medical museum in Edinburgh when I was a student. What today's scene of crimes officer would have made of Bannockburn. *Exactly* those injuries."

"Bannockburn? That's what? Fourteen hundred?"

"Thirteen fourteen."

"Bloody hell, Anya. This is a hotel. In Whitby. Half the town's chartered accountants are downstairs having their Christmas party. And you're telling me someone's walking along the upstairs corridor with William Wallace's cudgel? Taps on the door and says 'room service?'"

"I am. And Geoff will confirm it."

Another glance out of the window. The fog even thicker. If the back entrance to the hospital still existed Brady couldn't see it.

"You said it was a perfect crime scene. Or one that was too good to be true. What about blood pattern analysis?"

"Not just blood patterns. Splashes. Spatters. But blood patterns on white wallpaper. Like the hotel's interior designer knew there was going to be a murder."

Brady laughed. "Apart from the maroon carpet. What did it tell you?"

"It told me I'll need to do more analysis. With your permission I'd like to run the pictures past my old tutor. But the blood spatter... The angle of the blows. He was hit from above – "

"The first blow?"

"Yes. Right handed. Four or five inches taller than Hodge."

"What was Hodge? He looked about my size."

"Five ten. I'd say we're looking for someone over six foot."

"And right handed?"

She nodded again. "And fit. And... this sounds stupid. I'm ashamed of myself."

"Go on, tell me."

"That first blow. It wasn't easy. Hodge is moving, half-turning." Anya reached across Brady's desk. Picked up a report in a blue binder. Rolled it up. Got to her feet. "Stand up will you, boss?"

Brady did as she asked. Anya handed him the rolled up report. "You're four or five inches taller than me. Right handed. Hit me on the side of the head as I turn round."

She took a pace away from him. Turned so her back was towards him. Swivelled as though he'd spoken to her. Brady swung the report at her. Half-hearted, not wanting to hurt her.

The door opened. Frankie walked in. "That looks like constructive dismissal to me, DCI Brady."

Anya shook her head. Looked irritated by Frankie's comment. "It's a serious point, boss. That first blow isn't... He's not swinging his whole arm. The speed is coming from his wrist. Pass me the report."

Brady handed it to her. She took a step back. Held the report like she was holding a racquet. Hit him on the arm.

"Now imagine that with a cudgel," Anya said.

Brady rubbed his arm. "That hurt."

Anya smiled. "I was Scottish Schools' badminton champion. Like I say, it's all in the wrist."

"Right. Anything else?"

"No. I'll send the pictures of the blood patterns off if you're alright with it."

Brady nodded. "Thanks, Anya. Frankie, you want to tell me everything there is to know about Joe Hodge? Before we go and see Geoff? While I rub my arm..."

7

Frankie nodded at the curled-up report on Brady's desk. "Was it important?"

"The task force Kershaw's on. He said it was essential reading."

"Anya's put it to good use then."

"A disgraceful comment, Detective Sergeant. But remarkably accurate. What do we know about the late Mr Hodge?"

Frankie glanced down at her notes. "Joseph Peter Hodge. Engineering degree from Loughborough University. Worked for the same company for the last ten years. Your age, boss. You're the thirteenth? Hodge was October the first. So twelve days older than you."

"Twelve days of Christmas," Brady said. "Which we won't be seeing – "

"Unless we make some progress. Don't worry, you're not the only one who's got a date with a turkey."

"Sorry, Frankie. It's just... the timing. I hadn't realised how much I was looking forward to Christmas. What did I say to you the other day? We've filed all the paperwork in the 'it'll keep until New Year' drawer? We – "

"You put it a touch less delicately than that, boss."

Brady laughed. "I probably did. But a murder *won't* wait. So we need to lay Mr Hodge to rest as quickly as we can. Invite someone to spend Christmas in the custody wing at Durham. Sorry, you were saying…"

"He's divorced. Lives in Ponteland – it's just outside Newcastle, on the road to Jedburgh. As far as I can gather, on his own."

"Children?"

"One, a girl aged ten. Lives with her mum in Hexham. She's re-married."

"Someone's told her?"

"I spoke to Northumbria. Family Liaison Officer took care of it for us."

Brady nodded. "We'll need to speak to her. What was he doing in Whitby?"

"Exactly what the hotel said. Making sure the harbour wall stays the harbour wall. Structural stuff. Two or three days, twice a year."

"Always stays at Bagdale?"

Frankie nodded. "Like the manager said, one of their regulars. If twice a year counts as a regular."

"What about the rest of the time?"

"Other trips. Peterhead. Fraserburgh. Checking how the walls are reacting to the seawater. The salts, I suppose. But precautionary, mostly. The guy I checked with said the Romans were using concrete two thousand years ago. Used volcanic ash apparently. Said the structures were still intact."

"So the harbour's good for a while yet."

"Looks like it. Especially if we can find a volcano between here and Scarborough."

"Phone? Laptop?"

"Phone and an iPad. They're with the techies now."

"You tell them it was urgent?"

"I did. But there's that murder in York. We're in a queue. Clothes," she said. "Exactly what you'd expect for two days looking at a harbour wall in December. Practical, warm. None of the clothes brand new. He's probably got a 'harbour wall' overnight bag."

"His car? Anything interesting?"

"Golf GTI. Two years old. Plenty of miles. Trips to Peterhead and Fraserburgh presumably. Pair of walking boots in the back. Again, exactly what you'd expect."

Brady nodded. "Bathroom? Did you go through his toilet bag?"

Frankie raised her eyebrows. "Sorry," Brady said. "Tell me."

"Joe Hodge is disappointingly predictable. Toothbrush and razor not there – Anya had taken them for DNA. Everything else you'd expect. Shampoo. Tea tree and mint – "

"I'm getting old. I remember the days before shampoo had twenty different flavours."

" – A couple of grooming kits clearly nicked from previous hotels. Pair of nail clippers. Unopened packet of condoms. But a single guy – staying in Whitby just before Christmas..."

"Office parties? Poor bugger thinking he might get lucky?" Brady shook his head. Saw the blood-spattered walls. "Exactly what he *didn't* get. Let's go and see what Geoff has to say."

8

B rady pushed the door open. Smelled the familiar mix.

"Death and chemicals, Geoff. It never changes."

Geoff Oldroyd – blue scrubs, dark green, plastic apron – looked up. "If you say so, Mike. Twenty years since I noticed it."

"How's it going?"

"I'm done, Mike. Or as done as I'm going to be. Mr Hodge and assorted internal organs have been weighed, measured – definitely *not* found wanting in his case – put back together and committed to the fridge."

He reached up, stripped off the apron, walked across to the sink and started washing his hands. "But his head was like putting a jigsaw back together," he said over his shoulder. "One of those bloody difficult ones your retired aunt delighted in."

"What do you want to do, Geoff? Go through it in here or adjourn to the briefing room in the Black Horse? That alright with you, Frankie? Our colleague looks like a man who's earned a pint of Doom."

"Why don't we split it, Mike? Cold, hard facts in here. Wild speculation when Sue's pulled us a pint and poured Frankie a gin?"

"Frankie?"

She nodded. "I have to speak to Lochie's mother tonight. The official plans-for-Christmas phone call. So only one."

Brady reached for a stool. Offered it to Frankie. Pulled a second one forwards. "Fire away, Geoff."

"First things first, Mike. What I just said. Joe Hodge was a guy in good shape. Mid-forties, so obviously starting to deteriorate a bit – "

'Twelve days older than you, boss.'

Thanks, both of you...

" – But generally in good shape. Search his house you'll find trainers. Check his bank statements there'll be a gym membership. Heart, lungs, kidneys... All good. Better than good. He could probably have defended himself in a fight."

"But there wasn't a fight."

"No. What Anya said to you was right. The first blow knocked him down, the second and third killed him."

"Definitely three?"

Geoff nodded. "He was hit three times with a weapon that did two types of damage. Puncture wounds and blunt force. There's no way of being certain but what Anya said about a medieval bludgeon ticks the boxes."

"Anya called it a cudgel."

"Club, cudgel, bludgeon. Whatever you call it the end result was the same – "

"As the walls testify. You think Anya's right on that, Geoff?"

"The blood pattern? The person that hit him was four or five inches taller? Blood patterns on walls aren't my area of expertise. But yes. The injuries to the side of his head –

someone was hitting down. Or at least across. Definitely not up."

Brady nodded. Found himself rubbing his arm where Anya had hit him with the report.

"What about the time of death, Geoff?"

The pathologist shook his head. "Time of death's bloody difficult. You know hotel rooms. How hot some of them are."

"But..."

"You want a time. I'll give you a window. Between eleven and one."

"So midnight?"

"Between eleven and one, Mike. Unless it was a full moon, obviously."

Brady laughed. "We've ruled that one out, Geoff. I told Frankie. No ghosts, no ghouls, no vampires, no werewolves. Cold, hard evidence. And nothing *but* cold hard evidence."

"Then you're in the right place. Or you were. I'm ready for that pint you promised me."

"One last question," Brady said. "This is probably nothing. But I thought I could smell something. Other than blood..."

Geoff nodded. "Anya said the same. As soon as she walked in."

"Me too," Frankie said. "Aftershave maybe? That sort of smell."

Geoff nodded. "Like I said, Detective Chief Inspector. You're in the right place. It was Paco Rabanne."

Brady raised his eyebrows. "That's impressive, Geoff. Don't tell me you've got a test for different aftershaves?"

"Science is a wonderful thing, Mike. Or Anya found a bottle in the bathroom. Your round I think..."

. . .

BRADY PASSED Frankie a gin and tonic. Handed Geoff a pint of Doom Bar. Walked back to the bar for his own drink.

"What's that?"

"It's mineral water, Geoff. I have to go and collect Ash from Bean's. Jessica's, I should say. And... there's a fair chance I'm going to be awake tonight thinking about Joe Hodge. I've already missed the aftershave. I don't want to miss anything else."

"And Christmas is coming."

Brady nodded. "Assuming we catch this bugger. I was planning some time off. I don't want to be poring over DNA results on Christmas Day."

"Tomorrow if we're lucky," Geoff said. "I bought half a dozen tickets in the lottery. Glass by the side of the bed. Empty bottle of Budweiser in the bin. I'm not hopeful though – "

"Because..."

"Because I think Anya's right, Mike. I'm *certain* Anya's right."

"You think Hodge opened the door? Led the way into the room? Half turned, he's hit on the side of the head – "

"I do. And then my guess is the killer walked straight back out. So the only DNA we'll find will be from the unfortunate Mr Hodge."

Brady nodded. Hoped Geoff was wrong. Said a silent prayer.

"Frankie? Any thoughts at this stage?"

She nodded. "One. Well, plenty. But one significant thought."

And I bet it's the same one I'm having...

"Go on..."

"Someone knocks on his hotel room door late at night.

He gets up and answers the door. 'Room service?' It can't be room service because there'd be a record of it."

Brady nodded. "And with due respect to Bagdale Hall, this is Whitby. Not the penthouse at the Ritz. Where you *would* get room service at midnight."

"So it's someone he's expecting," Frankie said. "But not someone he knows that well. If it all."

Exactly, Frankie. Exactly...

Geoff held his hand up. "Hang on, Mike. Three blows to the head. I'm certain of that. How the hell do you make the leap to someone he didn't know that well?"

"He led the way into the room, Geoff. We know that because of the position of the first blow. Supposing someone comes to your front door? Supposing someone comes to *my* front door. Bean comes round for Ash – "

"I thought she was Jessica now?"

"Sorry, Frankie, she is. I open the door, let her walk past me. Shout upstairs to Ash. Kate's the same. My sister. I kiss her, let her walk past me into the hall. But what about someone I *don't* know well?"

"Like what?"

"Suppose someone comes round to fix the cooker, Geoff? Electrician? Plumber? The plumber comes round and I'm going to open the door. Then *I* lead the way into the house."

"Except a plumber doesn't knock on your front door at midnight."

"Clearly not. But you take my point. So what Frankie's saying – and she's right – is that it was someone Hodge knew. But not that well."

"Knew or was expecting," Frankie said. "And there's something else..."

"What's that?"

"The plumber comes to your house. You open the door, lead the way into the house."

"Why?"

"Because you're showing him something, Geoff. 'This is where the problem is.' In the kitchen. Up here in the bathroom."

Geoff Oldroyd looked sceptical. "I'm still not convinced."

"Frankie's right, Geoff. Supposing Hodge *is* expecting someone? Someone who's come to collect something?"

"Collect what?"

Brady shook his head. "God knows. Because whatever it was, it isn't there now."

9

Frankie stood up. "Christmas calls," she said. "Bring me up to date in the morning if you cover anything else, boss?

Brady nodded. "Will do. I'll keep Geoff company while he finishes his pint then I'm off to collect Ash."

"You're sure you don't want another, Mike? Or will that mean you're up all night?"

Brady laughed. "Is that a comment on my middle-aged bladder?"

Because I will be up all night, Geoff. Drinking tea and trying to work out why someone took a medieval cudgel to a man who was checking the harbour wall...

"I've a question," Brady said. "I should have asked it before."

"What's that?"

"What was Joe Hodge wearing? We found him in his tracksuit bottoms. Bare feet, no top. Was he wearing boxers? Anything else?"

Geoff Oldroyd shook his head. "You should have asked and I should have told you. No, he wasn't. Tracksuit bottoms.

Nothing else."

Is that unusual? I do it if I've just come out of the shower. What about other blokes? I've no idea. And does it mean anything? Again, no idea...

Geoff picked his glass up. Finished his pint. Paused. Made a decision.

"I've a question for you then, Mike. Not one I was going to ask in front of Frankie."

"And you're looking serious, Geoff. What is it?"

Geoff shook his head. "No, I'm not looking serious. I'm looking... I don't know what the word is. Confused? Sceptical? Both?"

"Go on..."

"When you were in that hotel room, Mike. Did you feel anything?"

Brady looked at him.

He is serious about this. What's wrong?

"Murder scenes are always... Now *I* don't know what the word is. I've seen photographers, scene of crime officers who treat it like just another day in the office. I'm not like that. I always feel something. But that's not what you mean is it?"

Geoff shook his head. "I'm a scientist, Mike. Facts, informed speculation when it's needed. But in that bedroom... Did you not feel the chill?"

"I thought you said the bedroom was warm? That's why time of death was difficult."

"It *was* warm. I don't mean that. You said you missed something. The aftershave. Like there was something else. That's what I felt. Something else."

"It's December, Geoff. Whitby. Next stop the Arctic Circle. Give or take Newcastle and Edinburgh. No wonder there was a chill. People coming and going downstairs. Doors open all the time. Bloody cold outside. It would have been suspicious if there hadn't been the occasional chill."

Geoff shook his head. "Not that type of chill. Just – it sounds stupid – a *feeling* of cold. Hanging in the air. Despite the heating. That's why I didn't want to say it in front of Frankie. Like I say, I'm a scientist. But there was a chill in that room. A hairs-on-the-back-of-your-neck chill. A some-one's-watching-me chill."

I didn't feel it. I was too busy looking at the back of Joe Hodge's head. What was left of the back of his head.

What did I say to Frankie? 'Cold, hard evidence.'

Or is this something else I'm missing?

"Have you heard the story of Browne Bushell?"

Brady shook his head. Tried not to laugh. "No, Geoff, I haven't. Isn't Brown Bushell what you drink when Sue's run out of Doom Bar?"

"Browne with an 'e,' Mike. A person's name. He was the owner of Bagdale Hall."

"Bagdale Hall we were at today?"

"How many are there in Whitby? Captain Browne Bushell declared for Parliament in the Civil War. Then he swapped sides. Saw the chance of a little private enterprise – piracy to be exact – on behalf of the King. And himself, no doubt. Then he saw which way the wind was blowing and switched back again. Or tried to. The Roundheads weren't having it. Guilty of treason. Beheaded."

"So the owner of Bagdale Hall was beheaded four hundred years ago. I can't see that it's relevant, Geoff."

"His ghost. His ghost haunts the place. Hotel guests wake up in the night saying there's someone next to the bed. That they hear heavy boots going up and down the stairs."

Brady nodded. "Are you saying that's what the chill was?"

"Maybe…"

That Joe Hodge woke up and found himself face-to-face with a Civil War pirate? Said the wrong thing about Oliver Cromwell and had his head caved in? That'll convince a jury…

"I didn't have you down for – "

"Someone who believed in ghosts? Neither did I, Mike. Neither did I. So the sooner you catch him the better. I like being a scientist. I like being dull. And safe…"

10

"Can't we get a restraining order, boss? Seize his passport?"

Brady finished his bacon sandwich. Screwed up the paper bag. Punched the air as it arced across his office and nestled in the bin.

"It's not the same, is it, Frankie? With the greatest possible respect to everywhere else we've tried, nothing comes close to Dave."

"Only three months until he's back. What did Geoff have to say?"

Do I tell her? 'I didn't want to say it in front of Frankie.' So no, I don't.

"Not too much, Frankie. Joe Hodge was wearing tracksuit bottoms – and only tracksuit bottoms."

"Suggesting he'd got out of bed to answer the door?"

Brady shook his head. "If he was expecting someone? If you're expecting someone you're dressed. Properly. I think he'd just come out of the shower. In fact – "

Brady reached for his phone. Opened contacts. Pressed *Anya*.

"Anya, Mike Brady. A question – "

"Can I get my breath back, boss?"

Brady waited. Heard the noise of a gym in the background. Felt guilty for interrupting her.

"Sorry, boss. I'm training for a half-marathon. What can I do for you?"

"Accept my apologies for a start."

Because here I am again. Obsessed with finding the killer. Oblivious to anyone else having a life...

"...And answer a simple question for me."

"If I can."

"You went into the bathroom. Found the bottle of Paco Rabanne. Was there any steam in the bathroom? Or was the shower still wet? Or both?"

She didn't reply immediately. "Maybe," she said after a pause. "The mirror wasn't steamed up. I remember looking in it. The shower? I couldn't be categoric. Not in a court of law. But..."

"Yes?"

"Two of the towels were damp. I took them both. The first case I ever worked on. He stuffed a towel into her mouth. That's how we caught him. I've probably got a thing about towels now."

"Brilliant. Thank you. And I'm sorry again. Good luck with the marathon."

"Half-marathon, boss."

Thirteen miles? It still sounds a long way to me...

"What did she say?" Frankie asked.

"She said the towels were wet. So that's my theory. He came out of the shower, put tracksuit bottoms on."

Frankie nodded. Looked at him. "I'm coming round to your house, boss. You know I'm coming. Do you answer the door wearing nothing but tracksuit bottoms? Your sister's coming round. Same question."

Brady didn't reply.

"There's only one person you'd answer the door to dressed like that. Siobhan."

"Are you saying Joe Hodge had a date?"

"More than that, boss. He didn't just have a date. After-shave, just his tracksuit bottoms, condoms in his toilet bag... No-one came to collect anything. Joe Hodge was expecting to have sex."

'There's only one person you'd answer the door to dressed like that.' You're right, Frankie. Apart from that time you came round...

"We need the DNA."

"More than the DNA, boss. We need his phone. And his iPad. Fuck York. Whatever's happened there it can't be more important than this."

Brady reached for his phone. "Leave it with me. Eleven. No later."

11

"Clearly you've got more power than you thought, boss. Ten minutes before the deadline. *And* an apology."

Is this it? A breakthrough? Or is Christmas cancelled?

"What've we got? Joseph Peter Hodge. Do we know his life story?"

Frankie nodded. "Pretty much. And we can forget the iPad. Joe Hodge used it exclusively for Netflix, slaughtering aliens and re-building the Roman Empire. His phone has everything we need to know."

Brady breathed a sigh of relief.

"More or less," Frankie added.

Shit...

"Tell me."

"He liked his tech. The latest iPhone. A hundred and twenty different apps – "

"A hundred and twenty? No-one has a hundred and twenty apps on their phone."

Frankie raised a sceptical eyebrow. "You might want to check tonight, boss. I thought it was a lot as well..."

"So what's hiding in among all these apps?"

"OK. His e-mails show nothing special. Work and personal. Exactly what you'd expect from work. Ditto for personal. His dad had just gone into care. Plenty of back and forth with the home. And with his brother and sister. Half e-mail, half WhatsApp."

Frankie reached forward, finished her coffee.

"Joe Hodge liked a bet. Betfair, a couple of bookies' apps on his phone. But nothing from his bank statements to suggest it was a problem. About a dozen games. An equal number of football sites. He was a Newcastle supporter."

"That's not a reason for murder. A Geordie Man United fan and we'd have our motive. Come on, Frankie. I know you. You're saving the best until last. What was it about the so-far-very-ordinary Mr Hodge that wasn't ordinary?"

"He had the Grindr app on his phone, boss."

"That's..."

"A gay dating app. *The* gay dating app."

'He's divorced. Lives just outside Newcastle. As far as I can gather on his own. A daughter, aged ten. Lives with her mum in Hexham. She's re-married.'

Is that why the marriage broke up? Who knows? And right now it isn't relevant...

"Are you going to save Christmas, Frankie? Tell me he had a date on Wednesday night? That he sent a text message about eleven-thirty? We've traced the phone? Someone who lives in Whitby? A five minute walk away?"

Frankie nodded. "He had a date, boss. He sent a message. We've traced the phone he sent it to. But I'm not going to save Christmas."

Brady looked out of the window.

Nothing but the bloody fog. For the thousandth day in a row. And now I have to tell Ash that Christmas is cancelled...

Sighed. Shook his head. "Let's have the bad news."

"He had a date. With someone called Tom Finney – "

"Like the footballer?"

"If you say so, boss."

"Hodge sent him a message?"

Frankie nodded. "Eleven thirty-five. So if Geoff's time of death is right Finney took twenty, maybe twenty-five minutes to get there."

"And then he murdered him. And now you're going to tell me we can't trace the phone."

"I am. A pay-as-you-go sim. Bought from Poundland that afternoon."

"And the phone's at the bottom of Whitby harbour."

"That would be my guess."

"Did... I'm clutching at straws now. Did Finney send him a photo? That's what you do before a date isn't it? On a dating app?"

Frankie coughed. "He certainly sent him a photo, boss. But not of his face."

She passed him the phone. Brady glanced at it.

"Christ, there's something to make a man feel inadequate."

"You could say. Definitely not a photo taken on a cold morning in Whitby. Still, it'll make for an interesting ID line-up..."

No picture that's any use. And Tom Finney won't be anything like his real name.

We don't know why Hodge was murdered. We're no nearer finding the killer.

'Inadequate' might be the right word...

"There's always the DNA, boss."

Brady shook his head. "Finney – God knows it's not his real name but it'll do for now – has made sure we can't trace the phone. And if the phone's lying at the bottom of the harbour Anya's medieval cudgel will be with it. He's not going to do us any favours, Frankie. We can forget about him having a drink from a glass. Brushing his teeth with the oh-so-convenient toothbrush. Deciding to comb his hair after he's turned Joe Hodge's head into a jigsaw puzzle."

"What did Geoff say? About the results?"

"As soon as they can. But we're behind York in the queue. I bloody hate this, Frankie. Waiting patiently. I'm not good at it. I need a blood pressure monitor in the office."

"A blood pressure monitor or an exercise bike, boss."

Brady shook his head. "I get plenty of exercise. I print Kershaw's e-mails then I tear them into shreds. What's that line from the war? 'They also serve who stand and wait?' That's me. Standing and waiting for the DNA results."

"First World War or Second, boss?"

"I don't know, Frankie. Second, I guess. Maybe even the Falklands. You clearly know the answer so I'll go with the Falklands."

"Milton, boss. Seventeenth century. Written when he was going blind."

"So not the Falklands?"

Frankie smiled. "Give or take three hundred years..."

"Go and do some paperwork, Detective Sergeant Thomson. Wait for the mills of the DNA gods to grind exceeding fine. Let's see what – "

"Small, boss. The mills of the Gods grind exceeding small."

Brady shook his head. "Christ, Frankie, is there anything you don't know?"

She nodded. Sighed. "Sadly, the same as you, boss. Who killed Joe Hodge. And – "

Stopped herself saying any more.

"What, Frankie?"

She shook her head. "Nothing. Nothing to do with the job, anyway."

"You want to – "

"No." She looked at Brady. Briefly held his eyes. "It's fine, Mike. Like you say, I'll do some paperwork."

"I'll tell you the minute I hear anything. The minute Geoff phones."

And if he doesn't phone with something positive we're screwed. Maybe I should fall asleep. Hope the Ghost of Christmas Past tells me who murdered Joe Hodge...

12

"Mike, I need to come up and see you. *Just* you."

"That sounds ominous, Geoff. What's happened?"

"Ominous might be the word. Just remember I told you I felt a chill in that bedroom. Speak kindly to the coffee machine for me. I'll see you in five minutes."

BRADY WALKED across to the coffee machine. Tapped it twice. Said, "It's for Geoff, not me." Knew it wouldn't make any difference.

"Boss?"

Frankie's question was implicit. "He's on his way."

"You want me to come in?"

Brady shook his head. "He wants to see me. 'I need to come up and see me. Just you.' Those were his exact words."

"That doesn't sound like good news."

"That's what I thought. And it's not like Geoff to be cryptic. There's probably some hold-up. Probably needs me to exercise this new authority I seem to have. Give the lab a bollocking. Don't worry. The minute I've spoken to Geoff I'll let you know..."

"DEDICATED TO FIGHTING CRIME? We should start with arresting whoever made that coffee machine." Geoff took another sip. Winced. "There was nothing on the glasses," he said. "The murderer didn't have a swig from the Budweiser bottle in the bin."

Brady felt his pulse quicken. "The way you're saying that... Don't tell me we've got a match?"

Geoff nodded. "We have. But don't rush me, Mike. I'm still trying to come to terms with it."

"What are you talking about, Geoff? 'Come to terms with it?' That sounds like someone we know."

A copper? One of the team? Don't tell me that, Geoff...

Geoff shook his head. "This won't be the last time I say this. Not by a long chalk. You – we – have got Anya to thank. We've got a DNA sample. From the towels. Specifically, the hand towel. He must have washed his hands. Get some blood off them. Dried them on the towel. And didn't take it away with him. Why? I don't know."

"The most likely explanation is that he didn't know, Geoff. Or he didn't have time. A noise in the corridor outside? Accountants' Christmas party? Mr Collinson from the audit department has finally got lucky?"

"You've interviewed them all?"

Brady nodded. "Jake and Dan have done it. Interviewed every bloody accountant in Whitby."

"Nothing?"

"Not a thing. But if you've got a match... Tell me we've got a match, Geoff."

He nodded. "I've got a DNA match for you, Mike."

Brady punched the air. "Brilliant, Geoff. Bloody brilliant. I can't tell you how much we need this. The phone was a complete dead-end. Brilliant..."

Looked at Geoff. Felt his elation disappear. "What's that expression mean, Geoff?"

The same expression he had in the Black Horse. Confused and sceptical. But something else. Frightened?

"It means I've got a DNA match for you. Like I said, thanks to Anya. You want the rest of the good news? He's from Whitby. You could have strolled down the road and arrested him."

"'Could have?' That's the past tense."

Geoff nodded. "We've got a DNA sample. We've got a match. That's the good news."

"What's the bad news?"

"The person we've got a DNA match with is dead. He died three years ago."

"MATTHEW TURNBULL," Geoff said. "Matthew Henry Turnbull. Aged forty-two, last known address in Church Street. Like I said, Mike, you could have walked round. Missing, presumed drowned."

"Where in Church Street?"

"One of the jet shops. Boulton's."

Brady felt the ground slip from under him.

"Say that again. And – "

Brady stood up. Walked to the door. "You're alright if I – "

Geoff nodded. "Bring her in."

Brady walked across to Frankie's desk. "Spare me a minute. Watch me die of embarrassment."

"Matthew Henry Turnbull." Geoff gave Frankie the details. "Last known address in Church Street. One of the jet shops. Boulton's."

"That's not possible," Brady said. "I was there. The day before the murder. Buying a Christmas present. I've still got the receipt in my pocket. Talking to his wife. She *wanted* to talk for God's sake – "

And she told me that her husband was dead.

'Fell off the pier. Drowned himself.'

"Now you're telling me his DNA was at the murder scene?"

Geoff nodded. "I am, Mike. And we both know the possibility of a chance match. Billions to one."

"I was talking to her. His wife. Widow. Sadie."

"You think she knows, boss?"

Brady shook his head. "No. That's my gut reaction – "

'I'd got his hair in a box. When I hear him start telling the story I'm supposed to set light to it. The things we do for love, eh, Michael Brady?'

The things we do for love. Does that include lying to me, Sadie?

"– But what the hell do I know? I was talking to her for God's sake."

"That's the third time you've said that, boss..."

"Sorry, Frankie. I'm in shock. I'm buying earrings off this woman. She's telling me her husband is dead. Now Geoff's telling me he's *not* dead."

"There's one obvious solution, boss."

"What's that?"

"Turnbull had an identical twin. The DNA would be identical."

Brady shook his head. "Would it? I thought they were

fractionally different. Changes in the womb after the egg has split?"

"About ninety-nine point nine," Geoff said. "Mike's right. Changes can happen in the womb."

Brady shook his head. "Ninety-nine, a hundred, I'm still not having it, Frankie. I talked to her for half an hour. She told me the story. She mentioned a brother. But he was a younger brother. Besides, she's a leap year baby. And she's married an identical twin? That must be about one in a million."

"So I can add 'convenient coincidences' to the list of things you don't believe in?"

Brady nodded. "You can. Leave identical twins to Miss Marple. We need someone over six foot who had a motive for murder. And vampires, werewolves, ghosts, ghouls and identical twins have nothing to do with it."

"So do you think she knows?"

"That her dead husband's reduced Joe Hodge's head to a jigsaw puzzle? How *can* she know? She'd be an accessory. Go to jail. Lose her business."

"She's convinced her husband's dead?"

Brady nodded. "If I'm any judge of character. Which I'm beginning to doubt." He paused. Looked at Geoff. "No chance of a mistake?"

"None, Mike. And yes, I asked them to double-check. But 'no' is the answer to your next question. I don't know why we have his DNA on file."

"Frankie? Does the name ring a bell? Or do we need to check the records?"

"Check, boss. Yes, it rings a bell, but vaguely. Whitby's a small town. Every bloody name rings a bell."

Brady turned to his computer. Tapped his password in. Accessed the records.

"Assault," he said. "Boxing Day, four years ago. A hundred and eighty hours community service. Dig me out all the details will you, Frankie?"

She nodded. "What are you going to do, boss?"

"We've a choice of two haven't we? We go in with a search warrant. Or I go back and talk to her. Supposing she *doesn't* know? We go in with a warrant – one if she knows something she won't talk. Two... I liked her. I don't think she knows. And it's Christmas. I don't want to ruin her business. I'll talk to her first. See what else she tells me."

Frankie smiled at him. "Might cost you another pair of earrings..."

Brady laughed. "Then it's a good job I've got a daughter."

13

"Boxing Day, boss. Like you said."

"What happened?"

Frankie spread her hands. "What always happens on Boxing Day? Too many pints? A few whisky chasers? There was a fight down by the harbour. Turnbull was arrested. Charged with common assault. Spent a night in the cells. Like you said, a hundred and eighty hours of community service."

"And his DNA on file."

Frankie nodded. "So he has a history of violence."

"Or *had* a history of violence. Exactly what Geoff said. Missing, presumed drowned."

"What happened?"

"There were no witnesses. Not to the actual event. No-one saw him go in the water. One guy said he was fishing on the pier. Realised he'd forgotten his flask of coffee. Said he'd had an argument with his wife and gone out in a hurry. He said hello to Turnbull as he walked towards the town – "

"He could have been going to Dave's."

Frankie nodded. "He could. Wherever he went when he

walked back Turnbull was gone. Everything else there. Rods, bait, sandwiches, flask – "

"So no argument with his wife? Sorry, Frankie."

"Everything there. Just no Matthew Turnbull."

"Was there a search?"

"Lifeboat, the works."

"But they never found the body?"

"No. Missing, presumed drowned."

Brady nodded. "So let's assume he *wasn't* drowned. Let's assume for some reason he decided to disappear. Where's he been living? What's he been using for money? Bloody hell, Frankie, if I was going to disappear my starting point wouldn't be jumping into the North Sea."

Brady tapped his middle finger on his desk. "We've got to catch him, Frankie. We can't have a madman with a medieval cudgel wandering round Whitby's hotels."

"A madman or a ghost, boss. Everyone knows the story of Bagdale Hall."

"What did I say? No ghosts, Frankie. Cold, hard evidence.'"

"And the only evidence we have is Turnbull's DNA."

"Right. And three questions. Where the hell is he? Why did he kill Joe Hodge? And is he going to kill again?"

Frankie met his eyes. "The last one. Yes, he is. He went to a lot of trouble. You don't buy a medieval murder weapon on Amazon. What happened to Joe Hodge wasn't spur of the moment, boss. It was planned. And… I think he enjoyed it."

"So we have to find him. And we're not going to do that by luck. Not with this fog and a thousand square miles of North Yorkshire Moors to hide in. We've got to outthink him. Work out what he's going to do – "

"Before he does it."

"Right. Or someone else is going to die."

14

———

"You're looking thoughtful, Michael Brady."

What do I give her? The flippant answer? Or the real answer? Ask her...

"What do you want, Siobhan? A joke? Or the truth?"

"From you? You know the answer. You don't have to ask."

Brady nodded. "Then I'm thinking about the pier. Even though I can't see it for the fog. Jimmy Gorse. Our fight on the pier. And I know what you're going to ask me – "

She shook her head. "No, I understand. You love the house. You love where it is."

"I do. I absolutely do. But sometimes... Sometimes I sit here and think."

"What do you think?"

"That he's not dead. That it was someone else's body Dan Keillor pulled out of the sea."

"But it wasn't."

"No, it wasn't. It's just... I don't know. You know that old saying? 'Someone stepped on your grave?' I had it the other day. In Church Street. If anyone steps on my grave I don't want it to be Jimmy Gorse. My own private ghost. And I wouldn't be as lucky a second time."

Siobhan stood up. Walked over to him. Pulled him to his feet. "Stop being silly, Mike. It's the fog. We're sitting in your lounge and we can't see across the road. It's getting to us all. Come to bed. Let me hold you."

BUT IT WAS NO GOOD.

Brady reached out a hand. Tilted his phone so he could see the time.

Eleven forty-five.

What time will I get to sleep? Two? Three?

Pointless. Bloody pointless...

He put his fingers to his lips. Rolled onto his left side. Touched the fingers to Siobhan's cheek. Slid gently out of bed. Tapped his phone. Found a t-shirt and his tracksuit bottoms by the light of the screen. Closed the bedroom door as quietly as he could.

Put his finger to his lips a second time. A very different gesture. "No, Archie. Be quiet... And *don't* get excited. It's the middle of the night. It's not walk time. Well, not for you..."

Is this it? The future? Buy a house, renovate it, have a balcony overlooking the harbour. Somewhere to sit and think when I can't sleep. And I start walking. Rolling out of bed in the middle of the night. Creeping out. Closing the door gently so I don't wake Ash. Or Siobhan. 'I couldn't sleep so I went for a walk at midnight.'

"This is stupid," Brady said out loud. "Only mad people do this," he told the deserted street.

Pulled his coat round him. Shivered in the fog. Carried on walking.

Mad people who'll be missing Christmas if they don't find the killer.

One or two houses still with lights on. Ordinary people getting ready for bed. Pre-Christmas tourists deciding what to do tomorrow. Checking the weather forecast.

Fog, mate...

Reached the end of Henrietta Street. Started to walk down Church Street, the cobbles glistening wet in the lamplight.

Don't slip. Don't fall over.

'Where's Mike Brady today?'

'A&E. Fell over apparently. Went out for a midnight walk in the fog...

Took half a dozen more steps. Changed his mind.

'The Barguest Coach. Pulled by headless horses. The passengers are the skeletons of dead sailors. On their way to pay their respects up at St Mary's.'

Turned round. Walked back to the 199 Steps.

The houses crowding in on his right.

No lights on. They've gone to bed earlier than Henrietta Street.

Brady looked up the Steps towards the churchyard.

'Not the churchyard, Dad. The graveyard.'

Heard a seagull screeching through the fog.

Half the street lights were out. Brady pulled his phone out of his back pocket. "Hey Siri, turn torch on."

Looked up. Saw a teenage couple coming down. Laughing. Holding hands. Felt embarrassed at being caught talking to his phone.

The light hadn't come on. Realised he'd forgotten to charge it.

Started up the Steps.

Stumbled in the dark. Pitched forward. Put his left hand

down to break his fall. Felt his right knee crack against the edge of a step.

Swore.

Pushed himself painfully to his feet. Flexed his knee twice. Three times. Swore again.

Finally found a pool of light spilling out from one of the cottages. Tried to walk more quickly. Almost heard the light click off. Was back in darkness.

Knew that someone was walking a couple of paces behind him.

'The passengers. Paying their respects at St Mary's.'

Felt their presence. Felt the hairs on the back of his neck stand up.

Waited for the tap on his shoulder.

Told himself not to be stupid.

Stopped. Turned round and looked.

Street lights reflecting off the fog. Pitch black where the lights were out.

Flexed his knee again. Started back up the steps.

Reached the top. Walked into the graveyard.

Could just make out the gravestones through the fog.

When was the last time I was here? Bill's funeral. The call from Dan Keillor.

'There's been some remains found on the Moors. Human remains. I'm up there now...'

The call that led me to Becky. To Alice. Meeting Ruby.

Meeting Ruby again the other morning.

Her story about the young nun. Bricked up in the walls of the Abbey.

Brady looked across to the Abbey. Where the Abbey should be. Saw nothing but the fog.

Ruby and her ghost. The woman in the shop. Geoff. Frankie.

'A ghost or a madman, boss.'

"There are no ghosts," Brady said out loud.

Limped painfully towards the top of the Steps. Took one last look at the gravestones.

Matthew Henry Turnbull.

Is there one for you, pal? There shouldn't be.

Because you're not dead.

And I'm going to find you.

'Rest in peace?' You can forget that...

15

"So did you, boss? Make any progress last night?"

Brady nodded. "I walked up to the graveyard at midnight. Told Turnbull I was coming for him."

Frankie stared at him. Shook her head. "That's not a rational thing to do, Mike. Prowling the streets in the dark. That's not normal. 'Feral' is probably the word we're looking for."

Frankie turned to go. Stopped. Changed her mind. "Are you alright, boss?"

"I'm fine, Frankie. Why?"

"I thought I saw you limping when you were getting a coffee. And you're wincing."

Brady flexed his right knee under the desk. Struggled to keep his expression neutral. "I'm fine, Frankie. Never better. I'm going to walk round and see Sadie Turnbull."

"So it's not the warrant?"

Brady shook his head. "No. Like I said yesterday, I'll talk to her. Even if it costs me another pair of earrings."

"Have you got five minutes before you go?"

"Sure. Of course I have. Nothing wrong is there?"

"You weren't the only one awake last night. There's something I want to show you."

Is this what she was going to say the other day?

'Nothing to do with the job. It's fine, Mike. Like you say, I'll do some paperwork.'

Has Frankie got some problems? 'Something I want to show you?' She's had a job offer. She's leaving...

FRANKIE OPENED THE OFFICE DOOR. Walked over to her desk. Came back holding two blue files.

Battered police files. So nothing personal. At least not for now.

Brady nodded at the files. "Relevant to Joe Hodge?"

Not that I need to ask. Judging by your expression, Frankie, very relevant. The same expression you had when you came to the house that night. When you'd worked out who Gina Foster really was.

"Rosie Hillyard," Frankie said, putting the two blue files on Brady's desk. "She was sixteen. Up by the Abbey with her boyfriend."

"Courting? To use the old-fashioned euphemism..."

"As you say, boss."

"What happened?"

"Someone attacked her."

"Her, or them?"

"Her. The boyfriend was behind a wall having a pee. Heard her scream. Came running back. She's lying on the floor. Someone's disappearing into the night."

"When did this happen?"

"Two years ago. The winter before you arrived."

"So Bill's still in charge?"

"Bill and Kershaw, yes. And they drop the case after about two weeks. No chance of a conviction. 'Bloody teenagers, probably smoking something.' I can still hear Kershaw saying it."

"You surprise me. But I can see his logic. It's dark, there's only one witness... Presumably Rosie didn't see anything?"

"No. She said she heard a noise. Half-turned. Sees someone. Screams. Then he's hit her – "

"What with? Is this connected, Frankie? You're not going to say Anya's medieval cudgel are you?"

"No. The best guess from Geoff and Henry was a stone. Or a brick. There was one found near the path. Same direction the attacker ran off."

"Anything on it? Skin? Blood?"

"If there was the rain washed it off. It poured down that night. All the next morning. I think it was found some time in the afternoon. So not even remotely conclusive."

"Rosie was alright? No lasting damage?"

"No. Stitches in the cut. She went away to college not long afterwards. I can find out where if you want it."

Brady shook his head. "No, you're fine. What about the second one?"

"Jim Jefferies. Retired fisherman. He was attacked in St Mary's Churchyard. And it's the same story."

"The attacker gets away? Or Bill and Kershaw don't do anything about it?"

"Both, boss. It's late at night – "

"What's a retired fisherman doing in a churchyard late at night? He should be at home in bed."

"It was their anniversary. The day he proposed to her. They'd been together for fifty years or so. He said that's what they always did. Went for a few drinks. Ate fish and chips with their fingers and then walked up the steps to the churchyard. Then he proposed to her again. Like he'd done every year for fifty years. How romantic is that?"

"Except..."

"Except someone attacked him. Them. Pushed his wife out of the way. Jim said he saw something flash white. Then it was round his neck. Strangling him."

"What saved him?"

"His wife. The council had been doing some work in the graveyard. A workman had left a spade behind. Pure luck. Three hundred gravestones. She's next to the only one with a spade propped up against it. She manages to hit the attacker with it. He runs off, her husband survives."

"But Kershaw dropped the case?"

"Neither of them got a good look at him. They gave us a one word description. 'Big.'"

"What about this 'something white?' Whatever Jim was being strangled with."

Frankie shook her head. "The attacker took it with him. Jim said it felt soft – "

"You interviewed him?"

Frankie nodded. "Interviewed him. Took the statement. But his heart wasn't in it. Both of them. 'I'm the lucky one. Lucky to be alive.' That was all he kept saying. He thought it felt like a silk scarf. Said their daughter had bought his wife one for Christmas. Said it felt the same. But like I say, boss, 'lucky to be alive' was all they cared about. And the same as Rosie. Kershaw wasn't interested."

Brady nodded. Stared out of the window at the fog.

Where did I propose to Grace? On holiday. Not in a graveyard that's for sure...

"When did this happen, Frankie?"

"Ten days after Rosie Hillyard, boss. A few months before you drove your car across the Moors."

Brady stood up. "Phone him for me will you, Frankie? Tell him I'd like to see him. Maybe just after lunch."

"What do you want me to do?"

Brady laughed. "Sorry, Frankie. Die of boredom probably. Check through all the statements from the accountants will you? See if Dan and Jake missed anything."

"While you spend the morning with Turnbull's widow? Remember it'll cost you another pair of earrings."

"Not immediately. What did we say yesterday? 'Where's he been living?' I've got a theory. So I'm going to see someone. I'll probably freeze to death. And it'll cost me cake, not earrings..."

16

Brady had met Magic a few months ago. Told about him by a homeless ex-serviceman he'd suspected of arson.

Not the most conventional introduction...

'He's called Magic Pockets. Fuck knows what his real name is. You'll find him on the seat halfway up Blue Bank. He likes the view. Or doing the graveyard at St Oswald's. Top of Lythe Bank. He wears a big old coat. With magic pockets.'

"December," Brady said from ten yards away. "Not a time to be working in a graveyard. Especially on a cliff top."

"Mr Brady," he said without turning round. He was on his knees, tidying a grave, obscuring the headstone.

What is it? Three months since I found him on the cliff top? A gap in the hedge. An abandoned outbuilding on a farm. Tarpaulin for one of his walls. A fire in the corner, a battered black kettle. Dried herbs hanging from the roof...

The tramp finished what he was doing. Slowly straightened up. Well over six foot. Turned to face Brady.

Hair even more matted than the last time I saw him.

Beard not trimmed. T-shirt, shirt, jumper, jacket, his oversized coat...

Brady lost count of the layers.

"How are you keeping, Magic? It's bloody cold. Especially in this fog."

"Bloody cold is right." He nodded at the grave he'd been tending. "But not as cold as where old Mother Miller is. Least I can do is get her an' her mates tidied up for Christmas."

"The once a year relatives?"

And how long is it since you went to see Grace?

"Aye. Kids dragged along in protest. Rather play on a computer than see their grandma."

Brady unslung his backpack. Unzipped it and pulled the flask out.

"I was beginning to think you'd forgotten."

"No bacon sandwich though," Brady said. "Dave's in Spain. I went to see Mrs Botham for you instead. Happy Christmas, Magic."

Brady handed him the fruit cake. Magic read the label. Nodded appreciatively. "Fruit soaked in pale ale? Doesn't come much better than that. Seat over by the window?"

Brady laughed. "Not that we'll see much. But yes, the seat by the window. Lead the way."

Magic Pockets walked along the gravel path. Turned off and picked his way between the gravestones. Found the seat on the cliff edge. Reached into one of the hundred pockets in his coat. Found a penknife. "Fancy a slice wi' your tea?"

Brady shook his head. "I'm good, thanks. Big breakfast."

I didn't. But you need the cake more than me...

"Don't let me stop you though."

Magic laughed. "You won't, don't worry. Got to have some compensation for losing my view."

Brady sat down on the seat. Unscrewed the flask and poured the tea. Handed Magic the cup and a sachet of sugar.

"You remembered, I'm impressed. Then again, it's your job to remember things about folk." He drank some tea. Ate half the slice of fruit cake in one bite.

"What can I do for you then, Mr Brady? Flask o' tea, fruit cake... Who are you looking for this time?"

Brady stared into the fog. Couldn't even see the edge of the cliff.

Someone who's been dead for three years...

"I don't know."

Magic shook his head. "Impress me by remembering the sugar. Then you don't know who you're looking for?"

"I do know. My age. Tall. Over six foot. Maybe as tall as you. And I think he's living rough. Maybe not around here all the time. But often enough. And definitely in the last week."

"Not seen anyone. I've not been sharing my shelter if that's what you mean."

"No. I meant if you'd heard anything. Seen anyone new. Or someone who's back after being away for a while. Might call himself Tom Finney."

Magic shook his head again. "Name means nowt. An' I've not seen anything. Not in this fog. Mostly been reading. Reading – an' tryin' to keep warm." He half-turned, looked at the graveyard. "Taking care of my customers n' all."

Brady sipped his tea.

It was always a longshot. But worth asking...

"Thanks anyway, Magic. Ring me if you hear anything, will you? You've still got my number?"

Magic patted one of his pockets. "Filing system never fails me. All that paper, keeps me warm n' all."

Brady stood up. Poured the rest of the tea into Magic's cup. "You take care, mate. And make sure you do keep warm. Eat another slice of cake. Then it'll fit in one of your pockets."

17

"I didn't expect to see you again. Not so soon anyway. I thought her birthday was in the summer?"

Brady nodded. "It is."

But we've found some DNA, Sadie. It matches your husband's. The husband that died three years ago. Whose ghost beat a man to death on Wednesday night.

But let's not go there right now...

Brady looked at his watch. "You mind if we talk for five minutes?"

"You want me to close the shop?"

Brady shook his head. "Not the week before Christmas. We'll take our chances shall we?"

She looked at him. Clearly unsure what he was going to say. "You've got an expression you don't often see on a man."

Brady didn't know if he should laugh. "What's that?"

"Most men only have three expressions. I want food. I want sex. Don't interrupt me I'm watching football. Yours is the fourth one. 'I'm serious.' I'm fairly certain you're not going to propose to me. So if it's serious..."

She came out from behind the counter. Reached out the

hand with the rose tattoo. Dropped the latch on the door. Flipped *Open* to *Closed*.

"There. Five minutes isn't going to make a difference in this bloody fog. Between the fog and Amazon everyone in Church Street is saying the same. Worst Christmas on record."

And I'm not going to improve it...

"Fire away, Mr Brady."

"Even coppers have year ends, Sadie. We're trying to get all our paperwork in order. Dotting a few Is and crossing a few Ts. Closing old files. I wanted to ask you a couple of questions about your husband's disappearance."

"And Mattie's a T you can cross is he? What do you want to know? What can I tell you that I haven't told people already?"

Brady looked at her. 'Why is a Detective Chief Inspector bothering with this?' That's the question you should be asking, Sadie. Or maybe you want the answers as much as I do...

"Tell me about the day he died. Your statement's in the file but – "

"You want to hear it from the horse's mouth?"

Brady smiled. "I'd have put it slightly more politely. But yes. I wasn't here when it happened." Spread his hands. Smiled again. "But he's lying on my desk now."

Sadie shrugged. "What's to tell? He went fishing. He didn't come back. I inherited a load of debt, a fishing rod and a cod so small he should have thrown it back."

"What was the weather like?"

"It's all in your report, Mr Brady. But the weather was fine. Dusk on a September evening. High tide. And an empty bottle of Johnnie Walker in his fishing box. As the coroner pointed out. More than once."

Brady shook his head. "That doesn't prove anything."

"Don't need proof do you? Mattie-boy goes fishing, Mattie-boy doesn't come home. Conclusion, Mattie-boy is in the sea."

"Mattie could have..." Brady spread his hands. Didn't want to say it out loud.

"Mattie could have run off with another woman? Disappeared to Spain? He was born and brought up in Whitby, Mr Brady. And he loved his fishing. Fishing and the ghost walk. Like I said before, he wasn't born to stand behind a counter."

"So you don't think – "

"I don't think. I *know*. He might have abandoned his wife. He wouldn't abandon his favourite rod. Or the pier. Or his two weeks on the River Tweed. His line got snagged on the ladder. The one on the sea wall. He climbed over to get it free. One of the lads told the inquest he'd seen him do it once before." She nodded. "An' he was a tight bastard was Mattie. I can see him doing it. Just a bit more difficult with a bottle of whisky inside you."

"They never found the body?"

Sadie shook her head. "Spring tide. God knows why it's called spring tide in autumn but there you are. Mattie went in at high tide. Next stop Denmark."

'Poor bloody Mally, floating down the coast.'

Brady was back in Sam Brownley's lounge. Hearing the story of the boat going down. How it took a week for her husband's body to come ashore.

'Every bloody crab from here to Hornsea taking a bite out of him. I'm in the morgue. And there's Mally, looking like special effects out of Pirates of the bloody Caribbean.'

But you didn't have that, Sadie...

"How did you..."

How the hell do I ask this delicately?

"It's none of my business, Sadie. It's nothing to do with the case. But... you know what happened to my wife. How did you – "

"How did I grieve? How did I carry on? Is that what you're asking me?"

Brady nodded. "Yes, I suppose I am. I'm sorry. I'm a man. I'm not good with feelings."

She shook her head. "Don't apologise. Because you do, don't you? How did *you* carry on? Because you do. Funeral was the hardest. Funeral without a body. That's a tough one. We had a memorial instead. Me an' a few friends on the pier. Seemed the best place.

Brady looked at her. Smiled. "I've had my five minutes. More than my five minutes. Thank you. And have a good Christmas."

She smiled back. Lifted one of her long, elegant fingers. Twirled a strand of hair. "You as well, Michael Brady."

18

B rady had meant to walk back to the police station.
Instead he was standing by the harbour. Down the flight of steps, the swing bridge to his left.

Where Frankie and I ate fish and chips last year. The blue and red Christmas lights reflecting off the water. Where I was standing in May. Waiting for Greg Chadwick to come back on Dreamweaver. And ten minutes later I was jumping into the North Sea...

Brady pulled his phone out of his pocket. "Frankie? I'm down at the harbour ... where we eat fish and chips ... I don't know. Maybe I think better when I'm next to water. Maybe we all do ... Five minutes is fine. Grab two coffees on the way will you?"

Looked out across the harbour. Up to where St Mary's and the Abbey would be. Thought that maybe, just maybe, the fog wasn't quite as thick.

Remembered his conversation with Kate. *'Christmas dinner for six. Ash, Siobhan and me. You, Doug and Lucy.'*

Knew he finally had some answers...

. . .

"I've been to see Sadie."

"And…"

"Three things, Frankie. One, she doesn't know anything. Two, her husband's not dead. Three, he killed Joe Hodge."

"You're certain?"

"Absolutely certain."

"Why?"

"Because he spent two weeks every year on the River Tweed. And because she had a memorial service for him."

"Even for you that's a leap of faith, boss."

Brady shook his head. "She said he was born and brought up in Whitby. Loved his fishing, loved the ghost walk. 'He might have abandoned his wife. He wouldn't abandon his favourite rod. Or the pier. Or his two weeks on the River Tweed.' Those were her exact words. What do you do on the Tweed, Frankie?"

"Fishing is clearly the correct answer – "

"*Fly* fishing. What did Anya say to us? That first blow? 'The speed came from his wrist.' You've seen people fly fishing – "

"If Lochie's family have their way I'll see a lot more…"

"Right." Brady held his right arm out. Held an imaginary fishing rod. Cocked his wrist. "It's the same, Frankie. You've seen them on the pier. Sea fishing you're using two arms to cast. Your whole body. Getting the line as far out as you can. Fly fishing – "

Brady brought his arm forward. Flicked his wrist. Cast his line into an imaginary river.

"You're in the wrong place, mate. An' you've lost your fishing rod!"

Brady turned, saw he'd attracted an audience of two pre-Christmas drunks. Grinned at them. "Maybe that's why I haven't caught anything..." Turned back to Frankie. "It's exactly the same."

"So he wasn't the school badminton champion."

"It doesn't matter, does it? He went fly-fishing. That first blow. It would have been easy for him. Flicks his wrist forward. Second nature."

"You said you were certain he wasn't dead. Then you said she had a memorial for him. That doesn't make sense."

Brady nodded. "It does, Frankie. He's missing, presumed drowned. She's convinced he's dead. She... I don't know, Frankie. How the hell does she deal with it? She has to get on with her life. She can't have a funeral. There's no body. But she has to do *something*. So she has a memorial service on the pier. Where he went in, probably."

"So she thinks he's dead. We don't. And the DNA's on our side. He killed Joe Hodge. *Why?* That's what I don't understand."

"When are families together, Frankie?"

"Christmas."

"Right. I've got Kate coming round, you're spending it with Lochie's family. Christmas, weddings and..."

Frankie looked at him. Shook her head, still not understanding. "Funerals."

"Sadie said she had a memorial. 'Me an' a few friends on the pier.' Absolutely no mention of his family. He had a brother. Two sisters."

'*By the end of the week there's four of them all sleeping in one room.*'

"I'm off to see a retired fisherman, Frankie. You go back to the office. Find out what happened to Turnbull's family. I'll have a bet with you. January's bacon sandwiches says they're all dead. And they died more than three years ago."

19

B rady looked along the street.

Every one of them would have been a fisherman's cottage.

How many are holiday lets now? Second homes?

A five minute walk to the harbour. Nearly all of them...

Knocked on the door. Heard footsteps. A muffled, "I'm coming."

The door opened. Brady couldn't stop himself smiling.

Grey hair spilling out from under a battered Breton cap. An unkempt grey beard.

Google images. 'Weather-beaten old fisherman.' A perfect match...

"Well there's only one of you so you're not Jehovah's Witness. Thanks for phoning ahead, Mr Brady. Gave me chance to turn daytime TV off. Pretend I've got summat to do."

Brady shook hands.

T-shirt, check shirt, a hoodie, a well-worn bodywarmer. He'd give Magic a run for his money...

"December," Jim Jefferies said, reading Brady's mind.

"Bloody cold, 'specially with this fog. An' I can't afford to turn the heating on. Not now there's just me."

"I thought..."

"You thought there was me n' the wife?" Jim shook his head. "She fought a brave fight. But cancer won in the end. February. Two in the afternoon. Two in the afternoon on the second day of the second month. My own personal Armistice Day."

"I'm sorry, I didn't know."

"Doesn't do to dwell." Jim gestured at a chair. "Sit yourself down. You'll be wanting a brew no doubt. An' if you don't I do."

"Anything I can do to help?"

Jim shook his head. "I'm pretty bloody helpless without her. But I can make a cup of tea. Open a packet of ginger nuts."

Brady sat down. Looked around the room. Did what he always did. Looked at the pictures first. A sixties bride and groom standing self-consciously outside the church. A few years later gazing down at a baby. Jim's wife toasting him with a glass of wine, a Mediterranean beach in the background.

He heard the noise of a tin falling on the floor. A muttered curse. Resisted the urge to get up and help.

"Here we are. Hope it's alright. An' sorry for the swearing. Dropped the biscuit tin. Bloody arthritis."

Brady laughed. "Don't worry, I've heard a lot worse."

Jim walked over to the mantelpiece. Picked up a pair of grey, fingerless gloves. "Arthritis gloves. Daughter bought them for me. Don't know if they do any good." He held his right hand up. "Broke a few bones in my time. That n' the North Sea. Hauling the nets in the cold an' wet."

"Hard life," Brady said.

Jim shook his head. "The best life. Wouldn't have changed a thing. Heading out of Whitby as the sun rises? Not knowing what you'll see? What you'll catch? I'd go back tomorrow morning."

Brady reached forward, picked his tea up. Knew Jim would expect him to eat at least two biscuits.

"I need to ask you about that night in the churchyard, Mr Jefferies."

"Jim. Call me Jim. An' I figured you would."

"It was two years ago..."

"Two years ago this week. I told your – what was she? Sergeant? A bonny lass – I told her everything."

Brady nodded. "I know. It's just sometimes – when time has passed – sometimes we see things differently. Remember them differently."

"Tradition," Jim said. "Always told the skipper I had to be ashore on the twentieth. Only missed it once in forty-nine years." He nodded at the photograph. "Cost me a foreign holiday to make up for it. Drove a hard bargain did Kath."

"You went for a few drinks..."

Jim shook his head. "Only a couple. Who's got the bladder they had when they were twenty? Not me, that's for sure. So a couple of drinks, fish and chips by the harbour. Lovely night it was. We could see all the stars. And then up the Steps. Slowly. The cancer had taken hold by then. We knew it'd be our last time."

Brady saw the old couple walking slowly up the 199 Steps to St Mary's. Saw Kath stopping to rest. Saw Jim waiting patiently. Taking her arm, telling her it wasn't much further.

'I'm the lucky one.'

You weren't talking about the attack were you, Jim...

"I'm sorry. It must have been hard for your wife."

Jim laughed. "She was a determined bugger. 'It's not going to beat me, Jim.' Day she didn't say that to me I knew the end wasn't far away."

"But you finally made it to the top..."

"We did, we did. First time we'd done it as a laugh. Well, you do if you live in Whitby, don't you? Another clear night. Full moon n' all. 'Let's go up to St Mary's,' she said. 'To the churchyard.' I was all for it. Well, I was a young lad. You know what I was thinking... But I'm up there with her. Suddenly got serious. I was off out to sea in the morning. Made me think. So I dropped to one knee, took her hand. Probably still had grease on my fingers from the fish and chips. 'Will you marry me, Kath Gilroy?' I said. She said yes. But we had to keep it a secret 'til I'd asked her dad. Bloody hell, he were a tartar were her dad. 'You'll need your own boat one day if you're going to marry my daughter.' Her mum used to wink at me behind his back. She could see we loved each other."

Brady was happy to let him talk. Knew he'd get the full story that way. Knew Jim needed to tell it in his own way.

"Then what happened, Jim?"

"What I told that lass of yours. This shape... From nowhere. He pushes Kath out of the way. She falls. Lucky not to hit her head on a gravestone. An' he has something round my neck. Soft. Silk, like I said in my statement. But tightening it. Then our lass stands up. Like – I'm ashamed to say it."

He looked across at her photograph.

"Sorry, sweetheart. Don't haunt me. Like one of them films, Mr Brady. Where you think the monster's dead and it's not. There she is with a spade in her hand. Fetches him a God-awful crack across the side of his head. I can still hear the noise. He half stumbles. Lets go of me. Runs off. Down the steps. Both of us forty years too old to run after him."

"So you didn't get a good look at him?"

Jim shook his head. "Big bugger. Black clothes. That's all I can say. It all happened so fast."

"You think he followed you up the steps?"

"No, I don't. Kath had to stop. Three or four times. That's what you do on the Steps, don't you? Stop an' look out to sea. Except it were dark. So we looked back instead. I could see what she were thinking. 'Last time I'll walk up here.' Broke my heart it did. But no, Mr Brady. Cold night in December? There was no-one daft enough to follow us up there."

So was he waiting for you? Or for anyone that turned up?

Brady nodded.

Reached forward for his cup. Glanced at their wedding photo.

Don't you worry, Kath. I'll find him...

"One last question, Jim, if I may."

"As many as you like, Mr Brady. There's a while yet 'til *Countdown*."

"While you were being attacked... Did he say anything? Anything at all?"

Jim took a deep breath. Looked at Kath's photo a second time.

He's asking her permission...

Nodded slowly. "He did. Eight words. And I can hear 'em as clearly as I can hear you. As clearly as I can hear that spade hitting his head."

"What were they?"

Another glance at the photo. "He said, 'This is for my granddad, you old bastard.'"

"You're sure? Those exact words."

Another nod. "Sure as I'm talking to you."

"Did you tell Frankie that? Detective Sergeant Thomson?"

She can't have missed it out of her report, surely?

Jim shook his head. "No. We talked about it. It was a Tuesday when your lass came round. Day like this. Foggy. Remember seeing the fog behind her when I opened the door. But it was a Tuesday. And Kath was due to start chemo Wednesday morning. She said not to. She said he'd be caught some other way. I think... I think she just wanted me focused on her. Looking back, I didn't realise how frightened she was. And who was I to argue? Wasn't me that spent the morning throwing up."

"So you kept quiet?"

"We did. 'Til now. Reckon she'd want me to tell you now."

Brady stood up. Shook hands. "Thank you. I appreciate you telling me." Nodded at Kath's photo. "Do you talk to her every day?"

Jim put a hand to his eye. "Every morning. Every night. An' when I'm at the harbour. Down by the boats."

"Tell her something from me." Brady blinked. Felt tears prick the back of his eyes. "Tell Kath I'll find him for you."

"Aye, I reckon you will. You're a determined looking bugger."

Brady smiled. Picked his coat up. Walked across to the door. Reached for the handle.

"You know what the hardest thing is?" Jim said. "About losing her?"

Being in bed on your own. Waking up at three in the morning and reaching out for her. That's what I always thought. Now? Now, Jim, it's feeling guilty. Feeling guilty about being in bed with someone else.

"No, I don't, Jim. But fifty years together. It's a long time..."

"Fifty-two all told. Hardest thing? What I've just done with you."

"Talking? Having no-one to talk to?"

Jim shook his head. "Taking her clothes to the charity shop. Cooking for one. Just my name on the Christmas cards. I'd thought of all that. Coped with it as best I could. Making a cup of tea in the morning. Mr Brady. Hardly needing to fill the kettle. Hadn't thought of that one. Six o'clock every morning. Like God tapping me on the shoulder. 'Your turn next, mate. Not long now.' You married are you, Mr Brady?"

The only person in Whitby who doesn't know my story...

"I was, Jim. My wife died. In an accident."

Jim Jefferies looked at him. "Take my advice. You're a young man. Find someone else. Find someone to fill the kettle for..."

Brady had meant to walk straight back to the police station.

Instead he'd carried on walking. Crossed the swing bridge.

Turned his collar up against the cold. Pulled his coat round him. Turned left into Church Street.

He glanced at the jet shop. Kept his eyes down as he passed the alley where Patrick had been murdered. For the second time in three days started walking up the 199 Steps. Winced with the pain in his knee.

Had no idea what he was hoping to find in the graveyard.

'This shape... From nowhere. Pushes Kath out of the way. An' he has something round my neck. Then our lass fetches him a God-awful crack across the side of the head. He runs off down the steps. Big bugger. Black clothes. 'This is for my granddad, you old bastard.'

Brady reached for his phone. Doubted he'd get a signal in the fog.

Had to revise his opinion of EE.

"What's this, Mr Brady? You want to come round again? You developed a sudden urge to watch *Countdown*? Or don't you have any biscuits in the police canteen?"

Brady laughed. "Neither, Jim. A couple of extra questions, that's all."

That I should have asked you before...

"The night you were attacked. Where did you go for your drink?"

"Black Horse in Church Street, Mr Brady. Do you know it?"

Only slightly...

"I do. Our pathologist sometimes needs a pint of Doom Bar after a dead body. I occasionally keep him company."

"Aye, she keeps a nice pint does Sue. Two questions, you said."

"While you were in there – did you tell anyone what you were doing?"

"I didn't stand in the middle of the pub and announce it if that's what you mean. But it wasn't a secret. We talked about it to a couple of folk. After all, we'd been doing it for forty-nine years..."

"Thanks, Jim. You take care. And happy Christmas."

"Aye. You n' all, Mr Brady."

Was Turnbull waiting for you, Jim? Specifically for you? I think he was...

Because he heard you. One of those nights in the pub. Realised your anniversary is the same date that his grandad died.

Smiled to himself.

Knew all he had to do was walk up to the graveyard and wait...

Brady picked his way carefully between the headstones. As he always did, looked down at the inscriptions.

Realised what he'd found.

Not the names. The dates.

It's all about the dates...

Nodded. Turned and limped down the 199 Steps.

Replayed the conversation with Jim as he walked back to the police station.

'Tell her something from me. Tell Kath I'll find him for you.'

'Aye, I reckon you will. You're a determined looking bugger.'

I am, Jim. And I keep my promises.

'YOU GO BACK *to the office, Frankie. Find out what happened to Turnbull's family. I'll have a bet with you. January's bacon sandwiches says they're all dead. And they died more than three years ago.'*

"So did I win, Frankie? You're buying the bacon sandwiches all through January?"

Frankie didn't reply.

Focused on her screen. Concentrating. Making notes on a yellow pad.

Brady glanced down. Saw names and dates.

Waited for her to finish. Finally turn to face him.

"The names and dates? Turnbull's brother? His two sisters?"

"There are three of them, boss. Four if you count Grandad. And I'm not sure we should be betting on them."

"They're – "

Frankie nodded. "You were right. They're all dead. But you lost your bet. What did you say to me the other day? What are the chances of her marrying someone with an identical twin? A lot more than the chances of her marrying someone whose brother and sisters all die. But that's what's happened."

Brady shook his head. "Why didn't Sadie tell me?"

"Because – "

"No, don't say it, Frankie. She didn't tell me because I didn't ask."

I'm getting soft in my old age. I liked her...

"I didn't want to cause her any more pain. And now Turnbull's going to do that. She's accepted he's dead. Come to terms with it. Now she's going to have to accept that she married a murderer."

"Only if we catch him, boss."

"We'll catch him, Frankie. I've made a promise. Go on, go through it for me."

"His sister's the first one. Vicky. She was asthmatic. A condition called eosinophilic asthma. Your body produces more white blood cells than it needs. Your airways become inflamed."

"And she died of an asthma attack?"

"She did. She'd had a cold apparently. Out walking the dog. Something triggered it. Busy road? Pollution? And then a year later Turnbull's brother. He's away on business. Dies of a brain aneurysm in his hotel room. His wife told the inquest he'd been complaining of headaches. Said he didn't have time to go to the doctor."

"Christ, this is grim. When?"

"The sister in twenty-twelve, the brother a year later."

"And the attacks start a year later. After Turnbull's disappeared. Who's left, the youngest sister?"

'That night Tilly – she's only four, she wasn't down there – she goes into her big sister's bedroom and says, 'Can I sleep with you, Vicky?' And by the end of the week there's four of them all sleeping in one room.'

"How did she die?"

"Her car burst into flames. She married an American.

Lived in Portland. She'd dropped her kids off at a party. Was driving home. Someone hit her at an intersection."

"And the car burst into flames?"

Frankie nodded. "Last year. Which is why you lose your bet. You want to read the report?"

Brady shook his head. "No. I probably want to buy more life cover. What about Grandad? Tell me he died peacefully in his bed."

"Not quite. But nothing so dramatic. He fell and broke his hip. Pneumonia."

"The old man's friend? He died in hospital?"

"No. At home. He refused to go into hospital. Wanted to be treated at home."

"What about Turnbull's parents? What would they be now? Late sixties? Early seventies?"

"In Spain. Inherited the shop from Grandad presumably. Sold it. Moved to Spain. So far, still alive..."

"And grieving..." Brady stared down at Frankie's notes.

'He used to do the ghost walks in the summer. Easter to Halloween. Always think of him when I walk down Grope Lane.'

"Are you going to say it or am I?"

"The connections?"

Brady nodded. "The connections with the ghosts. I meet Ruby. She tells me about Constance de Beverley bricked up in the walls of the Abbey."

"Where she must have died of asphyxiation."

"Which – God help her – must be more or less what happened to Turnbull's sister. Or what he imagined it was. His brother dies in a hotel."

"So does Joe Hodge. But his grandad doesn't fit the pattern."

Brady shook his head. "He can't copy every death,

Frankie. Not exactly. But he's had a bloody good try. And who's to say his grandad's funeral wasn't at St Mary's?"

"What's that leave us with?"

"He's ticked all the boxes. The Abbey, Bagdale Hall, the graveyard."

"Except two. The West Pier and Grape Lane"

"No. Turnbull's the West Pier. That's where he died. Supposedly died. Grape Lane. All that's left."

"Bloody hell, boss. This is real life *Cluedo*. Matthew Turnbull in Grape Lane – "

"With the flames. That's the only box he hasn't ticked. Grape Lane. The ghost of Mary Clark. And his little sister."

"And we're left with two questions. "Who? And when?"

Brady shook his head. "One question, Frankie. 'Who' doesn't matter. Because it's not going to be a random stranger. 'Who' is going to be one of us. And 'when' is easy. He attacked Jim Jefferies on the anniversary of his grandad's death. Check when Vicky died. It'll be the same date as the attack on Rosie. His brother will match Joe Hodge."

"And the date of Tilly's death – "

"Will be the date he tries to kill someone in Grape Lane."

Frankie looked down at her pad. Checked on her computer. Picked her pen up. Circled a date on the pad. Looked up at Brady. "She'd dropped her children at a Christmas party. December the twenty-second. Tomorrow."

"TOMORROW?"

Frankie nodded. "Tomorrow, boss."

So no sleep tonight...

"Boss... Just now... You said. 'It's not going to be a

random stranger. It's going to be one of us.' That sounds like you want a decoy. Or a target. Have I just volunteered?"

Brady shook his head. "No, Frankie. I had someone else in mind. I'm planning to give Turnbull exactly what he wants. I'm planning to give him Mary Clark."

"Except Mary Clark was a young girl."

Brady nodded. "And I haven't asked her yet. And she might say 'no.' She – "

"Anya?"

"Anya. And before you say it, Frankie, I know. She's a scene of crime officer. And Turnbull's a murderer. Who smashed Joe Hodge's skull. Who would have strangled Jim Jefferies. But this is Whitby."

"Who else have we got? It's her or me? And you want someone young."

"I do. But like I said, I haven't asked her yet."

21

What did you say to me, Anya? 'I've decided to live a long and healthy life.' And I want to use you as bait...

She didn't hesitate. Didn't ask Brady if it was going to be dangerous. Didn't ask 'why me?'

Simply said yes.

"You saw what Turnbull did to Joe Hodge."

Anya nodded. Looked Brady straight in the eye. "And that's why he has to be stopped."

Asked only two questions. "When..."

"Not until it's dark. Sunset is at three-thirty. But the light will last after that. Turnbull can't walk through Whitby in daylight. Or half-light. So from five. I'll have Dan Keillor and Jake and a couple of uniformed guys on duty through the day. But ghosts only come out at night. Everyone knows that."

...And "how?"

"My hair, boss. I've read the story. Mary Clark had 'long, golden hair flowing behind her.' My hair's as far from 'golden' as you can get."

"Don't worry. It will be. Frankie's pal works in the wardrobe department at the theatre in Scarborough. She says you won't quite be Rapunzel. But you won't be far off."

Anya smiled. "So Rapunzel whose dad was born in Mumbai? You think we'll get away with it?"

Brady nodded. "It's December, Anya. You'll have your collar turned up. And he'll be focused on your hair. Not your face..."

Now we come to it. The sentence I've been dreading...

"Frankie will make sure you're dressed properly. Fire resistant clothing. Everything we can possibly do. But – "

"But you can't do anything to protect my face. I'd already worked that out. But like I said. I saw the back of Joe Hodge's head. You definitely think he'll kill again?"

"I'm certain. More certain every day."

"So it's simple. We have to stop him." She looked at Brady. Nodded. "I'm ready, boss."

"Thank you. Those words aren't adequate – "

"But they're all you've got?"

"Pretty much. Hair, make-up, costume then. Tomorrow afternoon."

_____

22

"You want to come for a walk with me, Frankie?"

She raised her eyebrows. "I thought we had a killer to catch?"

"We do. That's why we're going for a walk."

"Where?"

"Grape Lane. Grape Lane in the dark and the fog. You know what the army say. 'Time spent in reconnaissance is never wasted.'"

"And you're getting nervous. You need to do something."

Brady laughed. "You know me too well. Grab your coat."

THEY CROSSED THE SWING BRIDGE. Turned right at the Dolphin.

Into Grape Lane. The Christmas lights blurred by the fog. Hazy reflections off the wet paving.

"Not much more than a hundred yards end to end," Brady said. "Two hundred at the most. I think Anya comes in from Church Street. Walks past the Captain Cook

Museum. You, me, Dan, Jake, a couple of uniforms. We can cover it."

"You're definitely not going to close the street?"

"No. Close the businesses early. I'll walk down in the morning and tell them. But leave Grape Lane open. However determined Turnbull is he's going to be put off if there's a copper at either end of the street. The rat has to walk into the trap, Frankie. The fish has to take the bait."

"It looks wrong," she said. "Christmas decorations in the shops. Trees, lights. People shopping. Holding hands. Those two…" She nodded at a couple ten yards in front of them, his arm round her shoulders. "What do you think? Their first Christmas together?"

"And you and me skulking along behind them with our dirty little secret?"

She nodded. "Something like that."

"Remember what I said to you once, Frankie? When we'd worked out who'd murdered Alice? 'Alice deserves justice,' I said. 'And it's up to us. Because this is who we are.'"

"I do. And I remember what I said to you. When we'd worked out who Gina Foster really was – "

"When *you'd* worked out who Gina really was."

"I said, 'This is as good as it gets isn't it?' And for me and you, it *is* as good as it gets. Right here. Right now."

"The anticipation? I looked down at those notes on your pad. The names, the dates. I knew we'd found him. All we have to do is wait for sunset."

Frankie laughed. "You make him sound like a vampire."

"Come on. Let's get back.

She put her hand on his arm. Stopped him. "You're sure, Mike?"

"Am *I* sure about tomorrow? Are *you* sure about the dates?"

"Yes, I am."

"Then I'm sure about tomorrow. What's the alternative, Frankie? We comb the Moors? Check every beach hut? We don't have the manpower."

"Are you sure about Anya? I could – "

"You could still do it? I know you could. I know you *would*. But Anya's the right choice for this. Am I sure about setting a trap? No, I'm bloody terrified. But it's the best option. We have to catch him. And that's what being the boss is. Making decisions. And sometimes it's a lonely place."

"And no-one else understands."

"You understand, Frankie."

"You're right, I do. I – " She broke off. Looked at Brady. "What are you doing?"

Brady was pulling on a black iron gate, an alley between two shops behind it. "Making sure it's locked. Sadie told me. Turnbull was doing the ghost walk once. She was hiding in an alley. Not tomorrow. Grape Lane's gates can stay locked."

"She doesn't know about this?"

"Absolutely not. She can stay safely behind her counter. Like I said, let's get back. It's getting even colder."

23

"Did you sleep?"

"No," Frankie said, "Not much. You?"

Brady shook his head. "But I didn't walk up to the graveyard at midnight. So maybe I'm making progress. Here." Brady put his hand in his coat pocket. Passed Frankie her breakfast. "There's a business opportunity for someone. Overcoat with an insulated pocket. Keep your bacon sandwich warm in winter – "

"Your beer cool in the summer? I'll phone *Dragon's Den* for you, boss."

"Are Dan and Jake in? I want to make sure they're well-rehearsed. Even if nothing happens."

The phone rang on Frankie's desk. She reached forward and picked it up. Listened briefly, handed it to Brady. Mouthed, "For you..."

"Michael Brady."

He recognised the voice at once. The faint lilt of Carlisle. Halfway between the North West and a soft Geordie accent.

"Magic, what can I do for you?"

"Well, bacon sandwich and a flask of that tea'd be a good start. Call in next time you're passing."

"I'll do that. But you didn't ring me about breakfast. Hopefully not..."

"You wanted to know if there was anyone new."

"I did."

"One of the lads was down the Seafarers' Mission. Heard someone say he'd gone to a shelter."

"A homeless shelter?"

"A shelter up on West Cliff. Where he normally sleeps. Said there was someone new up there. Told our lad to fuck off. 'Big bastard,' he said. 'Aggressive.'"

"Did he say when?"

"Two nights ago. One night's pretty much the same in a shelter. Not sure I even know what day it is. But yeah, two nights ago."

Does that mean he spent yesterday checking Grape Lane? Maybe. And the shelter on West Cliff to Bagdale Hall. What's that? Ten minutes?

"Thanks, Magic. Thanks very much indeed. You take care. I'll see you before Christmas."

And we'll have a whip round for the Seafarers' Mission as well...

"Good news?" Frankie said.

Brady nodded. "Like you said. December the twenty-second. He's here. It's today, Frankie."

MICHAEL BRADY LOOKED at his watch. Wondered if he'd broken the world record.

A hundred times today? And three trips to Grape Lane to confirm that nothing's happening. That Dan Keillor and Jake Cartwright are bored. That it's still cold. Still foggy...

Looked at his watch for the 101st time.

Two-thirty. Close enough.

Turned his computer off. Walked over to Frankie. "How's she doing?"

"I assume you're talking about Anya? A lot less nervous than you is the answer."

"Good. Hair and make-up?"

Frankie bent down. Picked up a box by her desk. "Hair, make-up and fireproof clothing. We'll see you at five, boss."

24

Two hoots on the car horn. The pre-arranged signal. 'We're here.'

Brady stepped out from the shelter of the Captain Cook Museum. Saw Frankie's Golf pull into the car park. Saw a flash of blonde hair in the front as a streetlight caught it. Watched her park. Get out of the car. Black leather jacket, black jeans. Walk round to the passenger door. Look up. Glance at Brady. Open the car door. Reach her hand out to Anya.

Brady shivered, pulled his coat round him. Spoke into the walkie-talkie. "Dan? Jake? All OK? They're here. Five minutes and we're good to go. Ten at the most."

Looked up and saw Anya.

A Bronte heroine. Cathy. Straight out of Wuthering Heights.

A long dress. Antique gold? Faded yellow? Frankie's pal has come up with a lot more than a wig.

She's Mary Clark...

Brady saw Frankie lean forward. Say something to Anya. Briefly take her hand.

Then leave her. Walk nonchalantly across to a shop. Idly look in the window.

While Anya started walking down Grape Lane...

She was holding the dress in her left hand. Full-length, with a tight waist. Her long, blonde hair cascading down her back as she walked.

Turnbull will think all his birthdays have come at once.

SHE WALKED PAST BRADY. Didn't even glance at him.

Five minutes to walk up and down Grape Lane. If that. How many times before it starts to look suspicious?

But Turnbull doesn't have a choice. He has to murder someone tonight...

"Fifteen minutes," Brady said into the walkie-talkie. "Do it in spells of fifteen minutes, Frankie. Then give her a rest. Put her in the car to warm up. I don't think Turnbull's watching. I think he's going to arrive, find a victim. He'll be banking on it being three days before Christmas. That it'll be busy."

"It could be a long night," Frankie said.

"It could be. But Turnbull doesn't have a choice. And neither do we."

'I'm training for a marathon, boss.'

Not the sort of marathon you had in mind, Anya...

IT WAS A LONG NIGHT.

Brady's 'spells of fifteen minutes' were down to ten minutes. The breaks in Frankie's car were getting longer.

Eleven o'clock. Six hours. I'm aching just from standing still. Exhausted from the stress. How the hell is Anya feeling?

'The twenty-second, boss. Tomorrow.'

There's not much of 'tomorrow' left, Frankie...

Brady reached for the walkie-talkie. "Half an hour, everyone. No more. Maybe he's waiting for closing time. Someone coming out of a pub, taking a short cut. That's our last hope. But eleven-thirty. And then we'll call it quits."

Because I can't ask any more of you. Not when I'm going to cancel your Christmas tomorrow morning.

'Happy Christmas. But there's a murderer on the loose. My genius idea didn't work. I've wasted everyone's time. And we're back to square one. So whatever plans you've made for the next few days...'

BRADY SIGHED. Shivered. Saw Anya climb out of Frankie's car for the final time.

Start walking down Grape Lane.

Walk past him, towards the Dolphin.

Then back again. Not many more times, Anya. 'And then we'll call it quits.'

Saw two people walking towards him.

A man and a woman.

He's two paces behind. Forcing her to walk in front of him.

Much bigger than her...

'Four or five inches taller than Hodge. I'd say we're looking for someone over six foot.'

'Big bugger, Mr Brady. Black clothes.'

All those and more.

And I know her.

Dear God. What the hell's happened?

"SADIE. WHAT ARE YOU DOING HERE?"

Mattie Turnbull took a pace to the right. Stepped out of the shadows.

Smiled at Brady.

Long, straggling hair, somehow thicker on one side than the other. Hooded eyes, dark, heavy eyebrows. An uneven beard. Tall, gaunt, ready for battle.

'Big bastard. Aggressive. Told one of our lads to fuck off.'

I'd say your lad had a narrow escape, Magic...

"I think Grape Lane's ready for another ghost don't you?" He pushed Sadie in the back. A step closer to Brady. "Tell him, sweetheart."

S he stared at Brady.

Angry. Accusing. Frightened.

"It's your own fault. 'Even coppers have year-ends.' My arse, Michael Brady. You over-egged your own pudding. I wasn't born yesterday. An' I got curious. There's been a murder, I say to myself. An' suddenly there's a copper back here asking questions. Not just any copper either. And I knew the dates. No doubt you looked them up. Worked it all out."

We did, Sadie. And spent a day congratulating ourselves. Or I did...

"That guy in the hotel. The same date as his brother. So that rings a bell. Then the girl, the one that got attacked up at the Abbey." She turned. Stared at Turnbull. "The one my late fucking husband attacked. And I think about Tilly. The date she died. *How* she died. So I put two and two together. And there's only one answer. I think to myself, this isn't coincidence, Sadie. Maybe it's time to take a walk down to Grape Lane. See if you really are a widow."

"And who does she bump into as she turns into Grape

Lane?" Turnbull laughed. Reached his left hand out. Grabbed a handful of Sadie's hair. Pulled her to him. Made her gasp.

"Here she is," he said. "My widow. Or my insurance policy. But you can have her."

He gestured behind him.

Anya was ten yards away.

A girl in a Victorian dress. The girl I put in danger. Long blonde hair cascading down her back. Standing outside a gift shop.

I can see her shivering from here. And not with the cold...

"She's the one I want. Prisoner exchange. Tell her to start walking towards me. And don't think about being a hero."

He brought his right hand up. Brady saw the light glint on the spikes. "There's not much you can't buy in the wrong end of Glasgow."

He flicked his wrist. Stopped the cudgel millimetres from Sadie's face. Smiled at Brady. "Hodge thought that. Turned when I spoke to him. Split-second when he thought he could be a hero. Then..." Turnbull shrugged. "Too late. But now you're not thinking it any more. So give me your girl. And you can have this one."

Come on, Brady. You're letting him dictate to you. Get some control.

"Take me instead," Brady said.

"Don't be bloody stupid. You're not a twelve year old girl. You think they're going to be satisfied with you?"

"Who? Who has to be satisfied?"

"The ghosts. Obviously."

How the hell do I answer that? He's mad.

"Anya isn't a twelve year old girl."

"No. But she's as close as I'm going to get. And you've gone to a lot of trouble. The dress. The wig. It'd be fucking rude of me not to appreciate it."

"You can't get away with this. I've men at both ends of the street."

Turnbull raised his head.

Like a dog. Sniffing the night air...

Shook his head. "No you haven't. You've got lads. I've seen them. I'm a big, ugly bastard. I'll take my chances."

"You'll be spending Christmas in Durham prison."

Turnbull shrugged. "What happens to me isn't important. But like I say, they're lads. And – "

"Do it, boss."

Anya's voice cut through the night. Cut through the fog. Cut through Brady's bargaining.

"No, Anya! No! Stand still! That's an order!"

She ignored him. Started walking towards Turnbull.

He turned. Saw her. Shoved Sadie hard in the middle of her back. Sent her sprawling into Brady.

Knocked him backwards.

Moved far more quickly than a big man was supposed to move.

Grabbed Anya. Crossed Grape Lane in two strides. Kicked a gate open.

The gate I tested yesterday. That was locked.

That isn't locked now...

Pushed Anya into the alley.

Brady scrambled to his feet.

It's still open...

Sprinted across Grape Lane.

Kicked the gate.

So hard it banged into the brick wall of the alley. Bounced back. Crashed into his shoulder.

Brady stood, gasping for breath, wincing with the pain.

He was at the top of the alley.

Barely wide enough for one person.

Felt something on his back.

Wind.

Wind off the sea.

Where the hell has that come from?

_____

Turnbull was four yards away. Five at the most.

Standing at the end of the alley. Light flickering behind him.

Anya slightly in front of him. Holding her with his left hand.

A bright red can in his right hand.

A petrol can. The same one I have in the car. More than enough to...

"Put that fucking can down, Turnbull. You're trapped. This can only end one way."

Turnbull nodded. "You're right. It can. 'Her hair had caught fire.' You know the story, Brady. They loved it on the ghost walk. 'Some say the baker beat the flames out. Some say she ran out into the street screaming, hair still on fire.' Me? I like the second version."

Brady saw him lift the petrol can. Pull Anya towards him. Tip the can. Start pouring.

Petrol splashing everywhere...

"Fuck's sake, Turnbull. Take me instead. Let her go."

He didn't reply. Shook his head.

Carried on pouring.

Anya looked straight at Brady. Met his eyes.

Nodded.

Took the long, flowing dress in her left hand. Lifted it.

Brady saw what she was wearing underneath.

Walking boots. Heavy, serious, walking boots...

She raised her left leg. Kicked backwards. Brady heard the crack as the boot made contact with Turnbull's shin.

It was enough. Just enough.

"Fuck! Fucking bitch!"

Brady darted forward. Yanked Anya free. Pushed her behind him.

Stood face to face with Turnbull.

"Take me instead? Is that what you said, pretty boy? Maybe I'll do just that."

Turnbull stepped forward.

Brady smelled the petrol. Saw the flickering light behind him.

Candles. Candles jammed into cracks in the old brickwork. There's another way into the alley. From the harbour. We never checked...

"Maybe I'll do just that," Turnbull said again. Raised his arm. Tipped the petrol can towards Brady.

Started pouring.

'Christmas Day. Dinner for six. Ash, Siobhan and me. You, Doug and Lucy.'

"Fuck you, Turnbull. I'm spending Christmas with my family."

Brady lowered his head.

Took a single pace forward.

Headbutted Turnbull in the centre of his chest.

Caught him by surprise. Saw him stagger. Take a pace backwards.

Stumble into the candles.

Saw the flames start.

WATCHED HORRIFIED as they leapt up.

Fascinated. Transfixed…

Heard Turnbull scream.

Brady wrenched his coat off.

Went to throw it over Turnbull.

No. You'll have to hold it over him. And you're covered in petrol.

"Turn round, you bastard! Turn round or you'll die."

Brady swung the coat. Swung it again. Heard Turnbull scream. Swung the coat three, four, five more times.

Finally realised the flames were out.

Watched Turnbull sink slowly to his knees.

Heard the ambulance siren.

Heard Sadie telling him the story.

'And they do say you can still smell the burning.'

I'll smell burning for the rest of my life, Sadie…

Michael Brady pulled the blanket round him. Smelled the petrol on his hands, his clothes. Decided he'd throw the clothes away.

"How is she, Frankie?"

"She's fine. Shaken, but she'll be fine. She's gone in the ambulance to be checked over. But she's tough."

"Dave with Jimmy Gorse. Anya with that bastard." Brady shook his head. "I don't know what to say. Hero. Heroine. They're not adequate."

"And you."

"No. Not a chance. I'm getting too old for this crap."

"You need to get those clothes off, boss."

"I know. You're right. But I draw the line at getting undressed in Grape Lane. Especially now the fog's gone. The wind – "

"Five minutes earlier and it'd have blown the candles out..."

Brady raised his hands to his face. "Christ, I stink. I'll walk home. Or walk to the station."

"The second one. Your clothes are probably evidence."

Brady looked back down the alley. "Big bugger was right," he said. "I'm going back to see Jim Jefferies tomorrow."

"Tell him you kept your promise?"

"More than that. A seventy year old woman hit that bastard round the head with a shovel? I'm going to tell him his wife deserved a medal. Another hero."

"There is some bad news, boss."

"What's that?"

"Your best coat. It's still smouldering."

Brady laughed. "It wasn't my best coat, Frankie. I've got more than one coat."

"It's the coat with the bacon sandwich pocket. That's close enough to best for me."

"I'll walk back to the station. Get these clothes off. Give Siobhan a call. 'Drive down to the station will you, love? Bring some clothes. Leave the cigarette lighter at home.'"

"Welcome to the world of dating a copper?"

"Something like that. You want to walk up with me? Or are you going home?"

"I'll walk home if it's alright with you, boss. Have a shower. Try and get the dirt off."

"Literal? Or metaphorical?"

"Both. The same as always. Then I'll drink gin at two in the morning. Think about Sadie Turnbull and the six stages of grief."

"I thought there was only five?"

"We've added a new one tonight. Anger, denial, bargaining, depression, acceptance. And number six. The bastard is back from the dead. Start all over again."

28

————

"What I can't get my head round is how he could do that to her. Run away. Disappear. Let her think he was dead."

Brady looked out of the window.

The fog completely gone. A pale winter sun. A few dark clouds on the horizon. Whitby. A normal winter's day...

"I shouldn't say this, Frankie. But I can usually find some sympathy for the killer. See their side of the story. Mattie Turnbull? None at all."

"Gina Foster?"

"I was thinking more of our friend in Crimdon. Her husband. What her daughter went through. But yeah, Gina as well. A victim – but two sides to her story."

"I still think about Gina," Frankie said. "One minute I hated her. The next I had total sympathy for her. And that's coming from a woman without children." She shook her head. "It's a bloody messy business we're in, boss. Where do you think Turnbull spent his gap year? His year off between attacks?"

"You want my guess? It'll be New Year before he can talk so we may as well speculate. My money's on Scotland."

"Salmon fishing in the Glennon?"

Brady looked at her. Narrowed his eyes. "Is that a joke, Detective Sergeant Thomson?"

"Enjoy it while you can. Two days' time you'll be relying on a Christmas cracker..."

"It's not the cracker that worries me. It's the hat. Ash will insist we wear hats. But yeah, that's my guess. A year in Scotland."

"I can see that. Obsessed with fishing. But if he's homeless and penniless where did he get a fishing rod? A permit?"

"I'll get Dan Keillor to check the records. Double or quits on the bacon sandwiches? There'll be a lonely fisherman attacked somewhere. Sitting on a riverbank unscrewing his flask. Looks up and Turnbull is standing over him. Permit?" Brady shrugged. "They can't patrol every river in Scotland can they? That's a lot of Scotland to patrol."

"Beautiful but deserted. Don't I know it."

Something about her tone of voice. If I'm ever going to ask, it's now...

"Is everything alright, Frankie? I got the feeling the other day... Is something bothering you? Tell me it's none of my business if you want. Put it more strongly. But..."

She shook her head. "No. And yes. Nothing I'm going to bother you with, Mike. Not for now."

'Boss' when it's work. 'Mike' when it's personal. So there is something...

"What about winter? Turnbull didn't stand on the banks of the Tweed through the winter."

"No, he didn't. One last guess? He went up to Fraser-burgh. Or Peterhead. Worked in the port. Found someone willing to pay cash. Maybe wasn't homeless and penniless..."

"And found out about Tilly."

Brady nodded. "She didn't come back for his memorial. Maybe he kept in touch with her. Swore her to secrecy. Or maybe he saw it online. You'd guess it was reported in her local paper. Either way it tips him over the edge. Convinces him that – I can't believe I'm saying this – convinces him the family is cursed."

"Says the man who doesn't believe in ghosts. Attacking people isn't enough? He has to do the job properly?"

Brady nodded. "Exactly that. Bloody hell, Frankie. Constance bricked up in the Abbey. Browne Bushell, Grape Lane, the lighthouse keeper. Tilly in America – "

"Far enough away to be safe. He must think that. But she still dies. And she's got children. Turnbull's niece and nephew. There's only one way to protect them..."

"Avenge everyone who's died. Which means Joe Hodge was just the beginning."

"You think he met Hodge up there, boss? Peterhead? Fraserburgh?"

"Found out he came to Whitby? Found out he'd be here on the day his brother died? Knew he stayed at Bagdale Hall? I'd say it was entirely possible..."

Frankie sighed. "Which explains what Joe was wearing. Or not wearing."

"Right. He'd met him through the app before. Something else Turnbull can tell us when he's fit to talk."

Brady's computer beeped. He glanced at it. Laughed. "Two days before Christmas. An e-mail from Kershaw. What do you think?"

"The same as you. Delete. End the year on a high."

Brady nodded. Reached across. Clicked his mouse.

Turned round. Looked at Frankie.

Do I say this? But if I can't say it to her...

"This case... I'm not sure I've covered myself in glory."

"Covered yourself in glory? Last night you damned near covered yourself in burning petrol." Frankie reached forward. Took his hand. Squeezed it. "You're a bloody good copper, Michael Brady. And a bloody good man."

Brady shook his head. "I'm getting soft in my old age. I should have been harder on Sadie. Asked more questions. I'd have got there sooner. Besides..."

He stood up. Reached for his coat. "There's something more important than being a bloody good copper."

"What's that?"

"Being a bloody good cook. Come on, Frankie, the fruit and veg shop is calling. And tomorrow I've an appointment with some sprouts. Parsnips. A potato peeler – "

"And I've an appointment with the A68." Frankie followed him to the door. "You have a good Christmas, boss. Give my love to Ash. Tell her I'll take her for coffee in the New Year."

"I will. And Frankie – "

"Boss?"

"Not 'boss.' Mike for this one. What you just said. 'A good copper.' Thank you. Your opinion..."

Frankie put her finger to her lips. Shook her head.

"Don't, Mike. You don't need to say any more. We both know."

29

Michael Brady dried his hands on a towel. Looked at the four pans on the hob.

"Sprouts, carrots, parsnips, potatoes. I'll be on *MasterChef* this time next year."

Siobhan laughed. "That was the easy part. Now all you have to do is bring it all together. On time. With the turkey. And the bread sauce. Roast potatoes..."

"Stop it. You'll give me nightmares. I need to sleep through the night."

"Don't forget to put your stocking out. And put some of that cream on your knee. Get the bruise out. You've had two days' sympathy. That's more than any man deserves."

Brady pulled her to him. Kissed her. "I'm sorry about tonight," he said.

She shook her head. Smiled at him. "No, it's fine. I understand. The first Christmas. Just the two of you."

What did Kate say? 'She's alright with that? Are you familiar with the word 'keeper?"

"I'll see you in the morning then?"

"You will. Bright and early. And bearing gifts. For Ash and Archie, obviously."

"Obviously..."

Brady kissed her again. "Come on, I'll walk you across –
"

"*Limp* me across the road..."

"Limp then. Hold the umbrella for you. It's bouncing off the cobbles."

Brady watched her rear lights disappear down Henrietta Street. Realised he was getting soaked, even under the umbrella. Turned round. Tried to look out to sea.

A month when I can't see the sea because of the fog.

Now it's the rain...

Heard the waves crashing remorselessly against the pier. Gave up and hobbled inside. Went upstairs to say goodnight to Ash.

"Gosh, Dad, you sound like Davy Jones coming up the stairs."

"Davy Jones? As in Davy Jones' locker? What are you talking about?"

Ash sighed her teenage sigh. "Davy Jones in *Pirates of the Caribbean*, Dad. Limping. Or Long John Silver to you. Are we still telling everyone you injured your knee the other night? Heroically saving Anya?"

Brady laughed. "If they'll believe it. I suspect my sister knows me too well."

He bent down and kissed her. "What are you reading now?"

"*Tess of the d'Urbervilles.* Completely depressing but no ghosts."

"No ghosts on a night like this. Even Dracula would stay on the ship tonight. Besides. I told you, Ash. They don't exist. No vampires, no werewolves. No ghouls."

And no ghosts. Not even knocking on the door of room 26...

"It's Christmas Eve. Where's your romance?" She looked at him. Held his eyes. "You sent Siobhan home. I'm sorry, Dad. She could have stayed. I wouldn't have minded. Really."

Brady shook his head. "No, not the first Christmas in the new house. Just you, me and Archie. So I'll wake you up at seven shall I? A long walk on a windswept beach."

"I'm a teenager, Dad. It's the holidays. Seven o'clock doesn't exist. Even on Christmas Day."

Brady laughed. Bent down and kissed her again. "Don't read for too long. And don't spend all night texting Jess."

Ash put her book down. "You think you did the right thing, Dad? Saving him?"

Brady nodded. "Joe Hodge has a family. They deserve... I was going to say 'justice.' They deserve an explanation."

"What about his wife? The woman in the jet shop?"

I go in to buy a pair of earrings. I end up taking her life apart...

"Honestly, Ash, I don't know. You'll find that out. War and crime. There are always casualties. Collateral damage. But did I do the right thing? Yes. Grape Lane's got enough ghosts."

"I thought you said you didn't believe in them?"

"I don't. You know what I mean. But no, I don't. There isn't Mary Clark in Grape Lane. There's no-one bricked up in the walls of the Abbey. There isn't a lighthouse keeper fighting to reach the lighthouse. Even on a night like this. So sleep well, sweetheart. And I'll see you on Christmas Day."

Michael Brady turned to leave. Heard the rain drumming against his daughter's window. The sea still pounding against the harbour wall.

Saw a small gap in her curtains. Walked over to pull them together.

Glanced out of the window towards the harbour and the West Pier.

WASN'T sure what he'd seen.

Looked again.

Is that a light on the pier?

Looked for a third time.

A light on the pier. Definitely. Appearing and disappearing through the rain.

Moving towards the lighthouse.

The lighthouse that isn't lit...

Brady stared through the rain.

The lighthouse on the West Pier isn't lit.

"Ash! Get out of bed. Come and look at this."

"What? I'm warm. I don't want to get out of bed. Unless you've seen Father Christmas."

Brady carried on staring.

There. Again. A light moving down the pier.

Slowly. Walking pace.

Towards the lighthouse...

"Ash, I'm serious. Come and look."

She sighed. Kicked her quilt back. Stood by his side.

"What am I looking at?"

"There on the pier. Where the lighthouse should be."

Ash shook her head sleepily. Didn't really look.

"Tell me again..."

"The lighthouse isn't lit. In a storm. And look down the pier. There's a light, moving towards it. Like someone's walking down the pier."

Brady glanced at his daughter. Looked back out of the window.

"What are you talking about, Dad? The lighthouse *is* lit. Red on one pier, green on the other. Like it always is."

Brady looked again. The lighthouse *was* lit. Like it always was...

"It was... I swear it was – "

"Can I get back into bed now, Dad? Now you've woken me up?"

"Yes, yes, of course you can. I swear, Ash – "

"What did you say, Dad? Two minutes ago. No ghosts. None in Grape Lane. None on the pier. Cold, hard evidence. That's what you *always* say."

She put her book down. Reached her hand towards her bedside light. "Sleep well, Dad. You're just tired. I said peeling all those potatoes would be too much for you."

Brady laughed. Blew her a kiss. Closed the door quietly.

WALKED DOWNSTAIRS TO THE LOUNGE. Stood at the French doors.

Stared at the lighthouse again.

But the rain had suddenly eased. The waves had dropped.

He looked across the harbour. At the pier, the lighthouse.

Lit, like it always is...

At Whitby.

The town he loved.

Christmas Eve. What's the line? 'How still we see thee lie.'
For now.
Until the next time...

REVIEWS & FUTURE WRITING PLANS

Thank you for reading *The Ghost of Grape Lane*. I really hope you enjoyed it.

If you did, could I ask you to leave a review on Amazon?

Reviews are important to me for three reasons. First of all, good reviews help to sell the book. Secondly, there are some review and book promotion sites that will only look at a book if it has a certain number of reviews and/or a certain ratio of 5* reviews. And lastly, reviews are feedback. Some writers ignore their reviews: I don't.

So I'd appreciate you taking five minutes to leave a review and thank you in advance to anyone who does so.

What next?

As it says in the 'Author Note' at the front of the book, *The Edge of Truth*, the fifth full-length book in the Brady series will be published at end of February. I'll then follow that with two more full-length Brady books later in 2023.

There are also two Michael Brady short reads/novellas, telling his back story in Greater Manchester Police from the time he first became a detective.

The Scars Don't Show tells the story of his first murder case. *Crossing the White Line* takes place roughly two years later.

If you'd like to receive regular updates on my writing – and previews of future books – you can join my mailing list via my website: www.markrichards.co.uk

SALT IN THE WOUNDS

His best friend has been murdered, his daughter's in danger.

There's only one answer. Going back to his old life.

The one that cost him his wife...

Salt in the Wounds is the first book in the Michael Brady series. It's available on Amazon and in paperback.

"Fabulous! Had me gripped from the start. Reminds me of Mark Billingham's detective, Tom Thorne."

"Loved the book from the first page. Straight into the story, very well-written. Roll on Brady 2."

"Loved everything about this book. A gripping plot with unexpected twists and turns. Believable characters that you feel you really know by the last page. I could smell the sea air in Whitby..."

THE RIVER RUNS DEEP

Good people do bad things
  Bad people do good things
  Sometimes it's hard to tell the difference...

Gina Foster's body has floated down the River Esk.

It looks like an accident. But Michael Brady has his doubts.

It's a year since his wife died. He's back in the police force, trying to prove himself to a new boss. And be a good dad to his teenage daughter.

Is it murder? Or does Brady need it to be murder?

Brady's convinced the answer lies in Gina's past. But his boss is doing everything he can to stop Brady finding out what that past was.

The River Runs Deep is the second book in the Michael Brady series. Again, it's available on Amazon and in paperback.

"Really love this crime series. Believable characters and good pace to the storylines."

"Another fabulous book. The characters are really developing, the story is well told and there are enough twists and turns and dead ends to keep you on your toes. Great new series to follow."

"The depth of the characters is so good I couldn't stop thinking about the story for weeks after I'd finished it."

THE ECHO OF BONES

"Find her for me, Mr Brady. I know she's dead. I know I'll never see her again. But find her. Give me a place to go on her birthday. Christmas Day. Somewhere I can take her teddy bear. Lay flowers. Find Alice for me, Mr Brady. Please..."

It's 20 years since Alice went missing.

There's never been any trace.

Until now.

Until some bones are found in a shallow grave on the cold, bleak North York Moors.

But is it Alice?

Or Becky? The other girl – who disappeared a month earlier...

Two local girls: two families that have finally learned to live with their grief.

But now Michael Brady must tell one family their daughter has been found.

And break the bad news to the other family.

No-one was ever convicted. Everyone's convinced the killer is in jail.

Everyone except Brady.

Brady has to re-open the old wounds. He has to find the real killer. And he has to stop seeing the similarities between his daughter and one of the murdered girls.

With the local families waiting for the 'killer' to come out of jail, with a boss determined to stop him discovering the truth – and without Frankie Thomson to help him – this is a case that affects Michael Brady like no other.

"Mike Brady is such a likeable character you want to become his friend, go for a drink with him or give him a hug when he obviously needs one. I've read all three Brady books within a week."

"Another Brady book I simply could not put down. Excellent story, brilliant dialogue. Had me hooked straight-away. And a real feeling of loss when it ended..."

CHOKE BACK THE TEARS

Michael Brady looked at Sandra Garrity's face. Grey skin. Bloodshot eyes open. Blue lips, her tongue protruding.

"Did you watch your husband die, Sandra? Or did he watch you die?"

"Brilliant. Brady is fast becoming the Yorkshire Rebus."

Billy and Sandra were childhood sweethearts.

Writing their names on a lovelock. Fastening it to the end of Whitby pier. Throwing the key into the sea.

A lifetime together. A happy retirement in a peaceful hamlet on the North Yorkshire Moors.

Until the day they were brutally murdered.

"Whoever did this – he didn't do it quickly. And he enjoyed it..."

Billy was a fisherman, making a living in the cold, cruel North Sea. One night his boat went down. Two crewmen drowned. Billy survived.

Are the families looking for revenge? It's the obvious conclusion.

But why have they waited so long?

Why have they killed Billy *and* Sandra?

And why kill them in such a barbaric way? 'This isn't a murder, Mike. It's an execution. A medieval execution.'

Choke Back the Tears is the fourth book in the Michael Brady series.

Kershaw's away, Brady's in charge. The bucks stops on his desk. But at least Frankie Thomson is back to help him. For now...

There are no clues. No motives. It's a perfect crime scene.

All Brady has is his experience and his intuition. And his small team is getting smaller by the day...

Meanwhile he's battling problems in his personal life. His daughter Ash wants to know the truth about her mother's death. Brady can't put off telling her any longer.

He's having doubts about everything.

Even the memory of his dead wife...

THE EDGE OF TRUTH

There are three sides to every story

Yours. Theirs. And the Truth.

Michael Brady is back. *The Edge of Truth* is the fifth book in the series. And there's a ghost from Brady's past...

'This series gets better and better and better.'

'Brilliant. Brady is fast becoming the Yorkshire Rebus.'

The push that sent Diane Macdonald over the cliff edge was surprisingly gentle.

She was walking her dog on the cliff top. Runswick Bay, a few miles north of Whitby.

Thirty-six hours later her body is found at the bottom of the cliff.

Brady's convinced it's murder.

But there's no evidence.

And only one witness.

Gerry Donoghue, a homeless ex-veteran. A man with a deep, dark secret.

And now he's disappeared.

Leaving Brady with Diane's husband, Graham Macdonald – the ghost from Brady's past.

"There was a crash. Lizzie died at the scene. Macdonald wasn't there. A crash that killed Lizzie, he escaped with a few bruises. The son of the Chief Constable was running away. Scampering across the fields, hand-in-hand with his guardian angel."

Twenty-five years later and Macdonald is an MP.

And a good friend of Brady's boss, Kershaw.

So there's pressure. Plenty of pressure.

And Michael Brady's not dealing with it very well.

He starts to make increasingly rash decisions – putting his personal and his professional relationships at risk.

But you know Brady by now.

He won't let it go.

He *can't* let it go...

The *Edge of Truth* will be published at the end of February 2023. You can pre-order the e-book on Amazon.

JOIN THE TEAM

If you enjoy my writing, and you would like to be more actively involved, I have a Reader Group on Facebook. The people in this group act as my advance readers, giving me feedback and constructive criticism. Sometimes you need someone to say, 'that part of the story just doesn't work' or 'you need to develop that character more.'

In return for helping, the members of the group receive previews, updates and exclusive content and the chance to take part in the occasional competitions I run for them. If you'd like to help in that way, then search for 'Mark Richards: Writer' on Facebook and ask to join.

ACKNOWLEDGMENTS

As always I'd like to thank my Reader Group on Facebook for their support, encouragement and help with the proofreading.

But my biggest thanks, not for the first time, go to my wife, Beverley, for her advice, insight, plot suggestions and – most importantly – patience. Being married to a writer is not an easy task...

Mark Richards
    December 2022

Printed in Great Britain
by Amazon